RETOLD TALES SERIES

RETOLD AMERICAN CLASSICS
VOLUME I

RETOLD AMERICAN CLASSICS
VOLUME 2

RETOLD BRITISH CLASSICS

RETOLD WORLD CLASSICS

The Perfection Form Company, Logan, Iowa 51546

CONTRIBUTING WRITERS

Michael A. Benware
B.A. English
English Teacher

Barbara L. Croft
Ph.D. English
Educational Writer

Debra Diane Felton
B.A. Communications
Educational Writer

Robert A. Klimowski
M.A. Reading, B.A. English
English Teacher

Beth Obermiller
M.A. English
Educational Writer

Michele Price
B.A. Communications
Educational Writer

Kristen L. Wagner
B.A. English
English Teacher

Mary J. Wagner
M.S. Reading, B.A. English
Reading Coordinator

FIELD TESTERS

Jon Ekstrand
Des Moines Alternative High
   School
Des Moines, Iowa

Janis Erwin
Kirby Junior High School
San Antonia, Texas

Ken Holmes
Lincoln High School
East St. Louis, Illinois

Gretchen Kauffman
Lincoln High School
Des Moines, Iowa

Michal Reed
Bartlett Junior High School
Springville, California

RETOLD TALES SERIES

RETOLD AMERICAN CLASSICS

VOLUME I

THE PERFECTION FORM COMPANY

Editors:
Kathy Myers
Beth Obermiller

Cover Art: Craig Bissell
Book Design: Craig Bissell
Inside Illustration: Paul Micich

TABLE
OF CONTENTS

WELCOME TO THE RETOLD AMERICAN CLASSICS

Gone with the Wind, a '57 Chevy, blue jeans, and *Louie, Louie*. What do this movie, car, piece of clothing, and song have in common? They're all great American classics.

We call something a classic when it is so well loved that it is saved and passed down to new generations. Classics have been around for a long time, but they're not dusty or out of date. That's because they are brought back to life by each new person who sees and enjoys them.

The *Retold American Classics* are stories written years ago that continue to entertain or influence today. The tales offer exciting plots, important themes, fascinating characters, and powerful language. They are stories that many people have loved to hear and share with one another.

RETOLD UPDATE

This book presents a collection of eight adapted classics. All the colorful, gripping, or comic details of the original stories are here. But longer sentences and paragraphs in the stories have been split up. And some old words have been replaced with modern language.

In addition, a word list has been added at the beginning of each story to make reading easier. Each word defined on that list is printed in dark type within the story. If you forget a word while you're reading, just check the list to review the definition.

You'll also see footnotes at the bottom of some story pages. These notes identify people or places, explain ideas, or even let you in on an author's joke.

Finally, at the end of each tale you'll find a little information about the author. These revealing and sometimes amusing facts will give you insight into a writer's life and work.

When you read the Retold Tales, you bring each story back to life in today's world. We hope you'll discover why the Retold Tales have earned the right to be called American Classics.

THE BLACK CAT

EDGAR ALLAN POE

VOCABULARY PREVIEW

Below is a list of words that appear in the story. Read the list and get to know the words before you start the story.

atrocity—terrible, cruel crime or act
bravado—boasting
carcass—dead body
deliberately—on purpose
despair—hopelessness
disposition—one's nature and temper
dread—fear
fatal—deadly
fragments—pieces
immortal—everlasting
interference—something that hinders or blocks
irritable—touchy; easily bothered
loathing—hatred and disgust
neglected—failed to care for or do
perverseness—to stubbornly turn away from what is good
remorse—deep regret
superstition—belief in something without proof or logical reason
supreme—highest or greatest possible
torment—torture
unburden—relieve

THE BLACK CAT

The narrator of this story has been sentenced to die on the next day. How can this have happened to a gentle man whose favorite hobby is raising pets? His bloody crimes begin after a mysterious black cat enters his life — a cat that may have the soul of a devil.

I do not expect or ask anyone to believe the wild yet ordinary story I am about to write. I would be mad indeed to expect it. Even I cannot believe what happened. Yet I am not mad—and I know I am not dreaming. But tomorrow I die, and today I hope to **unburden** my soul.

My main purpose is to tell the world about a series of everyday events. I tell the story plainly, briefly, and without comment. The results of these events have terrified—have tortured—have destroyed me.

Yet I will not try to explain these events. To me, they have brought nothing except horror. But to many,

EDGAR ALLAN POE

they will seem more odd than terrifying. Perhaps later some-one else will find a way to see my nightmare as ordinary. Such a person would be more calm, more logical, and far less excitable than I am. I describe these events with fear and wonder. Another might see them as just a common series of very natural causes and effects.

From the time I was an infant, I was known for my obedient and kind **disposition**. I was so tenderhearted that my friends made fun of me.

I was most fond of animals, and my parents gave me a great variety of pets. I spent most of my time with these animals. I was never happier than when I was feeding and petting them.

As I grew, so did my love of animals. As an adult, it was one of my main sources of pleasure. To those who have loved a faithful and wise dog, I do not need to explain how much happiness animals can bring. Something about their unselfish love goes right to the heart. This is especially true for one who has often been disappointed by the weak friendship and loyalty of *humans*.

I married young. I was happy to find that my wife's disposition was like mine. Seeing that I loved pets, she never passed up a chance to get the nicest kind. We had birds, goldfish, a fine dog, rabbits, a small monkey, and a *cat*.

This cat was very large and beautiful. It was entirely black and wise beyond belief.

Deep down, my wife was filled with more than a little **superstition**. She often mentioned the old belief that black cats are witches in disguise. Of course, she was never *serious* about this. I only mention the matter because I just now remembered it.

Pluto—this was the cat's name—was my favorite pet and playmate. Only I fed him, and he followed me all over the house. I even had a hard time keeping him from following me through the streets.

Our friendship lasted like this for several years. During this time, my personality completely changed for the worse. I am ashamed to admit it. This change happened thanks to the help of the Demon Alcohol.

Day by day, I grew more moody and **irritable**. I cared less and less about other people's feelings. I swore at my wife. Finally, I even treated her violently.

My pets, of course, felt the change in my disposition. I not only **neglected** them, but abused them. I still cared enough about Pluto to keep from mistreating him. But I did not worry about mistreating the rabbits, the monkey, or even the dog. It did not matter if they came near me by accident or for affection.

My disease grew worse—for there is no disease like alcoholism! Finally even Pluto, who was growing old and cranky, began to suffer from my bad temper.

One night I came home drunk from one of the places I often visited in town. I imagined that the cat was avoiding me. I grabbed him. My violence frightened him, and he nipped my hand.

The fury of a demon instantly possessed me. I did not know myself. My own soul seemed suddenly to fly from my body. A devilish hatred, fed by the gin, filled me.

I took a penknife from my vest pocket, opened it, and grabbed the poor cat by the throat. Then I **deliberately** cut one of its eyes from the socket! I blush, I burn, I shudder while I write about this damnable **atrocity**.

The next morning I could think more clearly, since I had slept off the drunkenness of the night before. I felt half horrified and half sorry for my crime.

It was a weak and mixed feeling at best. I did not regret it deep down in my soul. I began to drink too much again. Soon I drowned the memory of what I had done in wine.

In the meantime the cat slowly recovered. It is true that the socket of the lost eye looked frightful. Yet he no longer seemed to be in any pain. He went about the house as usual. But, as might be expected, he fled in terror when I came near.

Some of my old feelings still remained. So I felt hurt because the creature who once loved me now clearly disliked me. But soon this feeling changed to irritation. And then, as if to defeat me once and for all, came the spirit of **PERVERSENESS**.

No thought is given to this spirit. Yet just as I am sure that my soul lives, I am sure that perverseness is one of the basic urges of the human heart. It is one of the primary emotions that shape a person's character.

Who has not, a hundred times, found himself doing a shameful or stupid deed just because he knows he should *not*? Aren't we always inclined to disobey the *Law,* just because we know it is the law? And we do this in spite of our better judgment.

As I said, this spirit of perverseness finally defeated me. My soul longed to **torment** itself—to be violent to itself—to do wrong just for the sake of doing wrong.

This mysterious longing urged me to continue and finally to finish the injury to the innocent brute. One morning, in cold blood, I slipped a noose about its neck and hung it from the limb of a tree. I hung it with tears streaming from my eyes and with bitterest **remorse**.

I hung it *because* I knew that it had loved me and *because* I felt it had done nothing wrong. I hung it *because* I knew that I was committing a sin—a sin so deadly that I might risk losing my **immortal** soul. Even the Most Merciful and Most Fearful God might not be able to save me.

The night after I had done this most cruel deed, I was awakened by the cry of fire. The curtains around my bed were in flames. The whole house was blazing.

My wife, a servant, and I escaped from the raging fire with great difficulty. The destruction was complete.

Everything I owned was swallowed up. From that point on, I gave in to **despair**.

I am not so foolish as to look for a link between the disaster and my atrocity. But I am giving the details about a chain of facts. I do not wish to leave out any possible link.

On the day after the fire, I visited the ruins of my house. All of the walls except one had fallen in. This one wall was not very thick and stood in about the middle of the house. The head of my bed had rested against it.

For the most part, the plastering here had withstood the fire. I guessed that this was because the plaster had been spread recently.

A dense crowd of people were gathered around this wall. Many of them seemed to be examining a part of it very closely and eagerly. The words "strange!" "odd!" and other expressions made me curious. I came closer and saw in the white plaster the outline of a huge *cat*. It was amazing how accurate the image was. There was a rope about the animal's neck.

When I first saw this ghost—I could hardly consider it as any less—my wonder and my terror were extreme. As I thought about what must have happened, I was calmed. I remembered that the cat had been hung in a garden next to the house. When the fire was discovered, this garden had been filled immediately by the crowd. Someone must have cut down the animal from the tree. Then that person probably threw the body through an open window into my bedroom. This had probably been done to wake me up.

When the other walls fell, the cat's body had been pressed into the fresh plaster. Then the lime from the plaster, with the flames and *ammonia* from the **carcass**, had made the image I saw.

I reasoned through the events this way. But I was not completely satisfied. The startling image still made a deep impression on me. For months I could not forget the vision of the cat.

During this time, I felt something that seemed like remorse, but was not. I went so far as to regret the loss of the animal. In the disgusting places I often visited, I searched for another animal that looked the same to take its place.

One night I sat, half drunk, in a tavern known for wickedness. I suddenly saw a black object. It was lying on top of one of the huge barrels of gin or rum. These were the main pieces of furniture in the room. I had been staring at this barrel for some minutes. Therefore, I was surprised that I had not seen the object sooner.

I approached it and touched it with my hand. It was a black cat—a very large one. It was easily as large as Pluto and looked like him in every way but one. Pluto hadn't had a white hair on any part of his body. But this cat had a large, shapeless splotch of white. This splotch covered nearly all its breast.

When I touched him, he immediately stood up and purred loudly. He rubbed against my hand and seemed delighted with my attention.

This was the very creature I had been searching for. I offered at once to buy it from the landlord. He claimed it was not his—knew nothing about it—had never seen it before.

I continued to pet the animal. When I started to go home, it acted like it wanted to follow me. I let it do so. Sometimes I would stoop down and pat it as I walked.

When it reached the house, it made itself at home at once. It immediately became a great favorite with my wife.

As for me, I soon found myself disliking it. This was just the opposite of what I had expected. I do not know why, but its fondness for me disgusted and annoyed me. Slowly, these feelings of disgust and annoyance grew into bitter hatred. I avoided the creature.

A sense of shame and the memory of my former cruelty

kept me from physically abusing it. For some weeks, I did not strike or treat it violently. But gradually—very gradually—I came to view it with more **loathing** than words can tell. I fled silently when I saw it, as if from some terrible disease.

I had made a discovery that added to my hatred for the beast. On the morning after I brought it home, I found that it was missing an eye like Pluto. This only made my wife love the cat more. As I have already said, my wife was gentle and tenderhearted—as I had once been.

The more I hated this cat, though, the more it seemed to like me. I cannot describe how stubbornly it followed my footsteps. Whenever I sat down, it would crouch under my chair. Or it would spring up on my knees and smother me with its awful affection.

If I got up to walk, it would get between my feet and almost trip me. Or it would fasten its long, sharp claws in my clothes and climb up to my chest.

At these times, I longed to kill it with a single blow. I was kept from doing so, partly by the memory of my former crime. But mainly I was prevented—let me confess it at once—by my deep **dread** of the beast.

This was not exactly a dread of physical evil. Yet I do not know how else to explain it. Even now, in my prison cell, I am almost ashamed. It is difficult for me to admit why my terror and horror grew. It was one of the silliest ideas one could imagine.

My wife had called my attention, more than once, to the splotch of white hair I had mentioned. That was the only visible difference between this strange beast and the one I had destroyed.

The reader will remember that, though this mark was large, it had been shapeless. But slowly—so slowly that I thought I was imagining it—the outline had finally become very clear. It now looked like an object that I shudder to name.

This object, above all, made me hate and dread the monster. I would have gotten rid of it *had I dared*. The white patch was now the image of an awful—of a ghastly thing! It was the GALLOWS![1]—the sad and terrible machine of Horror and of Crime, of Agony and of Death!

And now I was truly miserable beyond the misery of ordinary humanity. Here was this *brute beast*—like the one I had destroyed—giving me such grief! *Me*—a man made in the image of God.

Alas! I could not rest by day or by night. During the day, the creature did not leave me alone. And at night, I awoke every hour from fearful dreams to find the hot breath of *the thing* upon my face. It was a living nightmare that I could not shake off—a huge weight forever upon my *heart*!

Under the pressure of these torments, the last little bit of good within me disappeared. Evil thoughts became my only friends—the darkest and most evil of thoughts. My usual moodiness increased until I hated everything and everyone. I did not even try to control my many sudden outbursts of anger. My uncomplaining wife was usually the victim of my fury.

One day she went with me on some household errand into the cellar. Because we were so poor, we were forced to live in an old building.

The cat followed me down the steep stairs. When it nearly tripped me, it enraged me to the point of madness.

I picked up an axe. In my anger, I forgot the childish fear that had kept me from doing this before. I aimed a blow at the animal. This blow, of course, would have been instantly **fatal** had it landed as I wished. But my wife jumped in and stopped the blow with her hand.

Her **interference** drove me into an evil rage. I jerked my arm from her grasp and buried the axe in her brain. She

---

[1]A gallows is a structure with a noose hanging from a crossbeam. It is used for hanging criminals.

fell dead on the spot without a groan.

This gruesome murder done, I began at once to think carefully of how to hide the body. I knew I could not take it out of the house either by day or by night. I would risk being seen by the neighbors.

Many ideas came to my mind. At one time, I thought of cutting the body into little **fragments** and destroying them by fire. At another time, I decided to dig a grave for the body in the floor of the cellar.

Again, I thought about throwing it in the well in the yard. Then I considered packing it in a box, as if it were a package to mail. I would get a delivery man to take it from the house.

Finally I hit upon what I considered a far better idea. I decided to wall the body up in the cellar, as the monks of the Middle Ages[2] are said to have walled up their victims.

The cellar was perfect for this purpose. Its walls were loosely built and had lately been plastered. The rough plaster had not hardened because the cellar was so damp.

Also a false chimney or fireplace jutted out from one of the walls. It had been filled up and made to look like the rest of the cellar. I was sure that I could easily take out the bricks from this place. I could insert the body and wall up the whole thing as it was before. I was certain I could do it so that no one who looked at the wall would suspect anything.

I was right about this plan. Using a crowbar, I easily removed the bricks. I carefully stood the body against the inner wall and propped it in place. I relaid the bricks as they had been before. With mortar, sand, and hair, I made a plaster just like the old. I very carefully went over the new brickwork with this mixture.

When I had finished, I felt satisfied that everything looked right. The wall gave no hint that it had been disturbed. I picked up the trash on the floor very carefully. I looked around with a feeling of success. Then I said to myself,

---

[2]The Middle Ages is a period in European history that lasted from about A.D. 500-1400.

"Here, at least, my labor has not been useless."

My next step was to look for the beast that had been the cause of so much misery. I had at last firmly decided to put it to death. There is no doubt what its fate would have been had I found it at the time. But the clever animal, it seemed, had been alarmed by my violence. It chose not to be around me in my present mood.

It is impossible to describe or imagine how happy and relieved I felt when the hateful creature was absent. It did not appear during the night. So I slept soundly and peacefully for the first time since the beast had followed me home. Yes, *slept,* even with the burden of murder on my soul.

The second and the third day passed. Still my tormentor did not come. Once again I began to feel like a free man. The monster, in terror, had fled the house forever! I would never see it again! My happiness was **supreme**!

The guilt of my dark deed hardly bothered me. A few questions had been asked, but I had easily answered them. A search had been started, but of course nothing was found. I thought my future happiness was safe.

On the fourth day after the murder, the police came to the house without warning. They started once more to carefully search the property. I was confident about the secrecy of my hiding place. I did not feel embarrassed at all.

The officers told me to come with them as they searched. They left no corner unexplored. Finally, for the third or fourth time, they went down into the cellar.

I did not tremble in the least. My heart beat as calmly as a person sleeping in innocence. I walked the cellar from end to end. I folded my arms on my chest and roamed easily around.

The police were completely satisfied and prepared to leave. My happiness was too strong to keep inside. I wanted to say even just one word in victory to make them more sure that I was not guilty.

"Gentlemen," I said at last, as they went up the stairs, "I am glad to have eased your doubts. May you all be healthy and a little more courteous.

"By the way, gentlemen, this—this is a very well-built house." (In the mad desire to say something casually, I hardly knew what I said at all.)

"I may say this is an *excellently* well-built house. These walls—are you going, gentlemen?—these walls are solidly built."

And here, through the excitement of **bravado**, I rapped my cane on the wall heavily. I hit the very spot of brickwork that hid my dead wife's body.

But may God protect and save me from the fangs of the Devil! No sooner had the echo of my blows faded than I was answered by a voice from within the tomb! It was a cry!

At first it was soft and broken, like the sobbing of a child. Then quickly it swelled into one long, loud, and continuous scream. It was totally unnatural and inhuman. It was a howl, a wailing shriek, half of horror and half of victory. Such a sound could have only come straight from the throats of the damned in hell and of the demons rejoicing at their pain.

It is foolish to speak of my own thoughts. Feeling faint, I staggered to the wall on the other side of the room. For one instant, the group on the stairs stood frozen in fear. Then a dozen strong arms tore at the wall. It fell.

There the corpse stood before our eyes. It was already greatly decayed and covered with gore. On its head, with an open, red mouth and one single eye of fire, sat the beast. It was the same horrible animal whose craft had tricked me into murder. Its voice had informed the police and condemned me to the hangman. I had walled the monster up within the tomb.

"The Black Cat" was first published in 1843.

INSIGHTS INTO
EDGAR ALLAN POE

(1809-1849)

Poe was the child of wandering actors. His mother died when he was two. His father simply disappeared. John Allan, a wealthy merchant, took Poe into his household. That's how Poe's middle name became Allan.

Poe invented the detective story. "The Purloined Letter" and "The Murders in the Rue Morgue" are two examples.

Poe is rumored to have had a serious drinking problem. The habit is said to have cost him job after job—even his life. Poe was found lying in a Baltimore street on October 3, 1849. He was unconscious and perhaps drunk. He died a few days later.

After Poe's death, one of his friends, Rufus Griswold, turned against him. Griswold changed some of Poe's letters to make the dead author look cruel. The plan helped sell Poe's books because the letters stirred up gossip. But it is hard to know what Poe was really like since Griswold twisted Poe's records. To this day, Poe's life has remained somewhat of a mystery.

Other works by Poe:
"The Cask of Amontillado," short story
"The Fall of the House of Usher," short story
"The Pit and the Pendulum," short story
"The Tell-Tale Heart," short story
"Annabel Lee," poem
"The Raven," poem
The Narrative of Arthur Gordon Pym, novel

THE CELEBRATED JUMPING FROG OF CALAVERAS COUNTY

MARK TWAIN

VOCABULARY PREVIEW

Below is a list of words that appear in the story. Read the list and get to know the words before you start the story.

absurd—foolish and silly
afflicted—troubled; bothered by pain
amateur—beginner; not a professional
ante—bet
buttonholed—cornered someone and forced them into conversation
calculated—figured or reckoned
celebrated—great and famous
circumstances—conditions
deliberate—careful; thought out
enterprising—energetic and determined in reaching a goal
exhorter—one who pleads or urges
garrulous—talkative
heave—the act of lifting or tossing something with difficulty
indifferent—not caring or interested
infinite—endless; limitless
limber—loose and flexible
monotonous—dull and filled with repetition
solitary—single
tedious—boring and tiring
tranquil—calm and peaceful

THE CELEBRATED JUMPING FROG OF CALAVERAS COUNTY

MARK TWAIN

JIM SMILEY LOVES TO BET, ESPECIALLY ON HIS FROG, DAN'L WEBSTER. NO WONDER. DAN'L WEBSTER IS THE BEST JUMPER IN THE COUNTY.

BUT A STRANGER DARES TO DOUBT THAT. HE CHALLENGES SMILEY TO A MATCH. AND SUDDENLY THE ODDS GROW *HEAVY* INDEED AGAINST THE CELEBRATED JUMPING FROG.

As a favor to a friend of mine from the East, I called on Simon Wheeler. Wheeler was a good-natured, **garrulous** old man. I was supposed to ask him about someone my friend had known—*Leonidas W.* Smiley. The result of my visit is the following tale.

Actually, I suspect that *Leonidas W.* Smiley was a

myth. I don't think my eastern friend ever knew such a person. My friend probably thought my question about Leonidas would remind Wheeler of the shady, well-known *Jim* Smiley.

My friend probably guessed that Wheeler would go to work and bore me to death with some bothersome stories about Jim Smiley. Those tales were sure to be about as long and **tedious** as they were useless to me. If that was his plan, it certainly succeeded.

I found Simon Wheeler dozing comfortably by the stove in an old run-down tavern in Angel's. Angel's was an old mining camp. I noticed that Wheeler was fat and bald. He had a nice gentle expression and simple look on his **tranquil** face.

He woke up from his doze and said good day. I told him that a friend had asked me to inquire about a good companion from boyhood days. This companion was named *Leonidas W*. Smiley—*Rev. Leonidas W*. Smiley, I added.

My friend had told me Smiley was a young minister. He was said to have lived in Angel's Camp at one time. I told Wheeler that I'd be grateful for any news of Rev. Leonidas W. Smiley.

Simon Wheeler backed me into a corner and blocked me with his chair. Then he sat me down and pulled up his own chair to block off my escape. Then he began to tell the **monotonous** story that follows.

Through it all, he never smiled, he never frowned. He never changed his voice from the gentle, flowing tone of the first sentence. He never showed a bit of enthusiasm either.

Instead, Wheeler told his never-ending story with great seriousness and sincerity. I saw that he did not think there was anything ridiculous or funny about his tale. Instead, he considered it as a really important matter. He said that the story's two heroes were outstanding geniuses in tricky scheming.

To me, the sight of a man calmly telling such a strange tale without smiling was wonderfully **absurd**. As I said before, I asked him to tell me about Rev. Leonidas W. Smiley. But I let him go on in his own way. In fact, I never interrupted him once. Here's the story he told:

There was a feller who lived here once by the name of *Jim* Smiley. It was in the winter of '49—or maybe the spring of '50. I don't remember which. But I do remember that the big flume[1] wasn't finished yet.

Anyway, he was the strangest man about always betting on anything that turned up. Anything that suited the other man would suit him. Just so long as he got to bet, *he* was satisfied. And he was lucky—uncommon lucky. He almost always came out a winner.

Smiley was always ready and looking for a chance to bet. Not a **solitary** thing could be mentioned that Smiley wouldn't offer to bet on. He'd take either side you pleased, as I was just telling you.

If there was a horserace, you'd find him rolling in money or broke at the end of it. If there was a dog-fight, he'd bet on it. If there was a cat-fight, he'd bet on it. If there was a chicken-fight, he'd bet on it. Why, if there were two birds sitting on a fence, Smiley would bet you which one would fly away first.

At camp meetings, he'd be there regular to bet on Parson Walker. (He judged the parson to be the best **exhorter** around here. And so he was, too, and a good man.)

Smiley would bet on a straddle bug. If he saw it start somewhere, he'd figure out how long it would take the bug to get wherever it was going. Once the bet was on, Smiley would foller that bug to Mexico. He'd do that just to find out where it was bound for and how long it was on the road.

Lots of the boys around here knew Smiley. They can tell you about him. Why, it never made no difference to *him*. He would bet on *anything*. He was the dangdest feller.

---

[1] A flume is a big ditch to drain water.

Parson Walker's wife got sick once. She was laid up for a good while. It seemed they weren't going to save her.

One morning, the parson came in here. Smiley asked him how she was. The parson said she was much better—thank the Lord for his **infinite** mercy.

"With the blessing of heaven, she'll get well yet," said the parson.

And, Smiley, before he thought, says, "Well, I'll risk two-and-a-half that she don't, anyway."

This here Smiley had a mare. The boys called her the fifteen-minute nag. But that was only in fun. She was a little faster than that. Smiley used to win money on that horse despite her condition. Besides being slow, she always had asthma or distemper or consumption[2] or something.

They used to give her two or three hundred yards head start, then pass her underway. But always at the tail end of the race, she'd get excited and desperate-like. Then she'd come prancing up, throwing her legs around in a **limber** way. Sometimes her legs would be up in the air and sometimes to one side among the fences.

She'd kick up m-o-r-e dust and raise m-o-r-e racket with her coughing and sneezing and blowing her nose. But she'd always end up at the finish line just about a neck ahead, as close as you could measure.

Smiley had a little small bulldog pup, too. To look at that pup, you'd think he wasn't worth a cent. You'd think all he did was set around and look ornery and wait for a chance to steal something.

But as soon as someone bet on him, he was a different dog. His lower jaw began to stick out like the top deck of a steamboat. His teeth would show and shine savagely, like furnaces.

Another dog might tackle him and bully and bite him. The other dog might even throw him over its shoulder two

---

[2]Asthma and consumption (tuberculosis) are illnesses which affect the lungs; distemper is an animal disease.

or three times. But, Andrew Jackson[3]—which was the name of the pup—would never let on that he wasn't satisfied. It was like he had expected nothing else.

Then the bets would be doubled and doubled again by the side against Andrew Jackson. They'd keep betting until all the money had been put up.

Then all of a sudden, Andrew Jackson would grab the other dog by the joint of its hind leg. He'd freeze there. Not claw, you understand. He'd only just grip and hang on till the other side throwed in the sponge, even if it took a year.

Smiley always came out the winner on that pup. But one day, Andrew Jackson came up against a dog that didn't have no hind legs. They'd been sawed off by a circular saw.

When the fight had gone far enough and all the money was bet, Andrew Jackson went to make a snatch for his pet hold. But he saw in a minute how he'd been take advantage of. The other dog had him.

Andrew Jackson appeared surprised. Then he looked sorta discouraged-like. He didn't try no more to win the fight. So he was beaten down bad.

He give Smiley a look as if to say his heart was broke. After all, it was *Smiley's* fault for putting him up against a dog with no hind legs to grab. That was the trick Andrew Jackson depended on in a fight. So Andrew Jackson limped off a piece and laid down and died.

He was a good pup, was that Andrew Jackson. He would have made a name for hisself if he'd lived. For the stuff was in him, and he had genius. I know because the dog hadn't no lucky breaks to speak of. It didn't stand to reason that a dog could fight like that under those **circumstances** if he hadn't no talent. It always makes me feel sorry to think of that last fight of his and the way it turned out.

Well, this here Smiley had rat-terriers and roosters and tomcats and all them kind of things. The list just went on

[3] Andrew Jackson was president of the United States from 1829-1837.

and on. And you couldn't fetch nothing for him to bet on but he'd match you.

One day he ketched a frog and took him home. Smiley said he **calculated** to educate him. So he never done nothing for three months but set in his back yard and learn that frog to jump.

And you bet he *did* learn him, too. He'd give him a little punch behind. The next minute, you'd see that frog whirling in the air like a doughnut. He'd turn one somersault or maybe a couple if he got a good start. Down he'd come, flat-footed and rightside up like a cat.

Smiley kept that frog in practice catching flies. He'd nail any fly within eyeshot every time. Smiley said all a frog wanted was education and he could do most anything— and I believe him.

Why, I've seen him set Dan'l Webster[4] down on this floor—Dan'l Webster was the name of the frog. He'd set him down and sing out, "Flies, Dan'l, flies!"

Quicker'n you could wink, Dan'l would spring straight up. He'd snatch a fly off the counter there. Then he'd flop down on the floor again, as solid as a gob of mud. He'd fall to scratching the side of his head with his hind foot. It was as if he didn't have no idea he'd been doing anything special more than any other frog. You never see a frog so modest and down-to-earth as he was, though he was so gifted.

When it came to fair-and-square jumping on a flat surface, Dan'l could get over more ground at one leap than any other frog. Jumping on a flat surface was his strong suit, you see. When it came to that, Smiley would **ante** up money on Dan'l as long as he had a red cent.

Smiley was horribly proud of his frog. And well he might be. Fellers that had traveled and been everywhere all said he topped any frog that ever *they* did see.

Smiley kept the beast in a little screened box. He used

[4]Daniel Webster (1782-1852) was a famous congressman and speaker.

to fetch him downtown sometimes and look for a bet. One day a feller—a stranger in camp, he was—came across Smiley with his box.

He says, "What might it be that you've got in that box?"

Smiley acted sorta **indifferent**-like. He says, "It might be a parrot. Or it might be a canary. But it ain't. It's only just a frog."

The feller took the box again and looked at it careful. He turned it round this way and that. He says, "H'm—so it is. Well, what's *he* good for?"

Smiley says, easy and careless, "Well, he's good for *one* thing, I should judge. He can outjump any frog in Calaveras County."

The feller took the box again. He took another long, careful look. Then he gives it back to Smiley. He says in a very **deliberate** way, "Well, I don't see no points 'bout that frog that's any better'n any other frog."

"Maybe you don't," Smiley says. "Maybe you understand frogs, and maybe you don't understand 'em. Maybe you've had experience, and maybe you ain't only a **amateur**. Anyways I've got *my* opinion. And I'll risk forty dollars that he can outjump any frog in Calaveras County."

The feller thought for a minute. Then he says kinda sad-like, "Well, I'm only a stranger here, and I ain't got no frog. But if I had a frog, I'd bet you."

And then Smiley says, "That's all right, that's all right. If you'll hold my box a minute, I'll go and get you a frog."

So the feller took the box and put up his forty dollars along with Smiley's. Then he set down to wait.

So he set there a good while thinking and thinking to hisself. Then he got the frog out and pried his mouth open. He took a teaspoon and filled the frog full of quail shot. He filled him pretty near up to his chin. Then he set him on the floor.

Smiley, he went to the swamp. He slopped around in the

mud for a long time, and finally he ketched a frog. He fetched him back and gave him to this feller.

"Now, if you're ready," says Smiley, "set your frog alongside Dan'l. Put his forepaws just even with Dan'l, and I'll give the word."

Then Smiley says, "One—two—three—jump!"

Smiley and the feller tapped the frogs from behind. The new frog hopped off. But Dan'l give a **heave** and hunched up his shoulders—like this, just like a Frenchman.

It wasn't no use—he couldn't budge. He was planted as solid as an anvil. He couldn't no more stir than if he was anchored to the spot.

Smiley was a good deal surprised and disgusted, too. But he didn't have no idea what the matter was, of course.

The feller took the money and started away. When he was going out the door, he sorta jerked his thumb over his shoulder at Dan'l. He says again, in that deliberate way, "Well, I don't see no points 'bout that frog that's any better'n any other frog."

Smiley, he stood scratching his head. He looked down at Dan'l for a long time.

At last he says, "I do wonder what in the world throwed this frog off. I wonder if there ain't something the matter with him. He appears to look mighty baggy, somehow."

Smiley ketched Dan'l by the nap of the neck and lifted him up. "Why, blame my cats, if he don't weigh five pounds!" he says.

He turned old Dan'l upside down. And that frog belched out a double handful of shot.

Then Smiley see how it was, and he was the maddest man. He set the frog down and took out after that feller. But he never ketched him. And—

Here Simon Wheeler heard his name called from the front yard. He got up to see what was wanted. Turning to me as he moved away, he said, "Just set where you are, stranger. Rest easy. I ain't going to be gone a second."

But, begging your pardon, I didn't feel much like hearing more about *Jim* Smiley. I did not think the history of this **enterprising** drifter would give me much information about Rev. *Leonidas W.* Smiley. So I started away.

At the door I met the friendly Wheeler returning. He **buttonholed** me and began again:

"Well, this here Smiley had a yellow, one-eyed cow that didn't have no tail. It only had jest a short stump like a banana, and—"

"Oh, hang Smiley and his **afflicted** cow!" I muttered good-naturedly. Telling the old gentleman good-day, I departed.

"The Celebrated Jumping Frog of Calaveras County" was first published in 1865.

INSIGHTS INTO
MARK TWAIN

(1835-1910)

Mark Twain's real name was Samuel Langhorne Clemens. He took "Mark Twain" as his pen name when he began writing humorous newspaper articles. The name probably came from a word riverboat pilots used to tell how deep the water was.

Mark Twain was born when Halley's Comet appeared in 1835. He predicted he would die when the comet came back near the Earth. (The comet approaches Earth about once every seventy-seven years.) Twain's guess proved correct.

Even as a young man learning the printing trade, Twain knew how to stir his readers. When the editor of his paper left for a week, Twain began publishing his own articles. The editor came back to find the town in an uproar over Twain's opinionated pieces. But Twain's stunt also won them thirty-three new subscribers.

Before becoming a fiction writer, Twain was a printer, steamboat pilot, reporter, and lecturer. He also was a silver miner for a time. Twain joined up with a partner to file a claim on some land. By law, they had to work on the claim within ten days or others could take the land. But Twain had to care for a sick friend and his partner was working another job. By the time they got back, their claim was legally in the hands of other miners. The lucky claim jumpers had discovered silver there worth millions of dollars.

continued

His name was known throughout the world. He was the most famous American alive. So when two men decided to write Mark Twain, they simply addressed their envelope, "Mark Twain, God Knows Where." They soon received a telegram from the author, reading: "He did."

Twain was an inventor and investor. He designed a notebook and scrapbook (the scrapbook sold over 100,000 copies a year). His investments were less successful. In fact, Twain's publishing house went bankrupt. Twain was not legally responsible for the debts. But he paid back every cent owed by going on an exhausting worldwide lecture tour.

Twain was known as a humorist. But especially in his later years, Twain's work and life turned bitter. Besides going bankrupt, Twain suffered the death of his wife and two daughters.

Huckleberry Finn was originally criticized as being too indecent for young readers. Even in this century, the book has been censored and banned. Despite that fact, Twain's masterpiece has sold over twelve million copies.

Other works by Twain:
The Adventures of Huckleberry Finn, novel
The Adventures of Tom Sawyer, novel
A Connecticut Yankee in King Arthur's Court, novel
Life on the Mississippi, autobiography
"The Man That Corrupted Hadleyburg," short story

TO BUILD A FIRE

JACK LONDON

VOCABULARY PREVIEW

Below is a list of words that appear in the story. Read the list and get to know the words before you start the story.

automatically—done without thinking; done as a routine or habit

burrow—to dig down and snuggle in

devised—planned or designed

devoted—applied oneself to a specific task or purpose; dedicated

expose—to uncover or lay bare

floundered—stumbled and struggled

foundation—base

genuine—real; true

impression—an effect made on the mind

instinct—a natural urge to behave in a certain way, usually present from birth

intently—with great attention

nucleus—center of an object or collection

observant—watchful; quick to notice things

previous—coming before

sensation—feeling or impression

subtle—hard to see, sense, or understand; faint or slight

sufficient—enough

tremendous—very great

welfare—well-being; safety and happiness

yearned—longed or hungered for

TO BUILD A

FIRE

The day was dawning cold and gray, extremely cold and gray. At this moment, the man turned aside from the main Yukon[1] trail and climbed the high earthbank. Here a dim and little-traveled trail led east through the forest of fat spruce trees.

Seventy-five below zero. That's how cold it is when the man in this story sets out to hike to another camp. In the lonely, dangerous land of the far north, the man has only a dog for company. One of them won't make it to the end of the trail.

[1]The Yukon is a river in Alaska and Canada that served as a major trail in the 1800s and early 1900s.

JACK LONDON

It was a steep bank, so the man paused for breath at the top. He excused himself for stopping by looking at his watch. It was nine o'clock. There was no sun nor hint of sun. But neither was there a cloud in the sky. It was a clear day, yet there was an invisible shadow over things. A **subtle** gloom made the day dark. That was due to the absence of the sun.

This fact did not worry the man. He was used to the lack of sun. It had been days since he had seen it. He knew a few more days must pass before that cheerful globe would peep just above skyline and immediately dip back down.

The man threw a look back along the way he had come. The Yukon River lay a mile wide and hidden under three feet of ice. On top of this ice was three feet of snow. It was all pure white, frozen into gentle waves from the ice jams.

As far as he could see north and south, the snow was totally white. Only one dark, thin line broke the whiteness. This line curved and twisted from around the spruce-covered island to the south. Then it curved and twisted away into the north. Finally the line disappeared behind another spruce-covered island.

This dark, thin line was the main trail. It led south five hundred miles to the Chilcoot Pass, Dyea, and salt water. The trail also led north seventy miles to Dawson. Still further north, it ran a thousand miles to Nulato. Finally it came to St. Michael, on the Bering Sea, fifteen hundred miles more.

But all this made no **impression** on the man. The mysterious, far-reaching trail; the absence of sun from the sky; the **tremendous** cold; and the strangeness of it all did not affect him.

It was not because he was used to it. He was a newcomer in the land—a *chechaquo*.[2] This was his first winter.

The trouble with him was that he had no imagination. He was quick and alert about things in life, but only in the things. He did not understand the meaning of things. Fifty

[2]Chechaquo is an Eskimo word meaning "greenhorn" (an inexperienced person).

degrees below zero meant about eighty degrees of frost.

This fact struck the man as meaning only that it was cold and uncomfortable. That was all. It did not lead him to think about how frail he was when it came to temperature. Nor did he think about man's frailty in general, able to live only within certain narrow limits of heat and cold. He also did not consider life after death and man's place in the universe.

To him, fifty degrees below zero meant frostbite that hurt. This must be guarded against by using mittens, ear flaps, warm moccasins, and thick socks.

Fifty degrees below zero was to him just exactly fifty degrees below zero. That there should be more to it than that never entered his head.

As he turned to go on, the man spat as an experiment. There was a sharp, explosive crackle that startled him. He spat again. And again before it could fall to the snow, the spit crackled in the air.

He knew that at fifty below, spit crackled on the snow. But this spit had crackled in the air. Undoubtedly it was colder than fifty below. How much colder he did not know.

But the temperature did not matter. He was headed for the old claim[3] on the left fork of Henderson Creek. The boys were there already. They had come across the divide from the Indian Creek country. He had come the round-about way. He wanted to check the possibilities of getting out logs from the islands in the Yukon this spring.

He would be in camp by six o'clock. True, it would be a bit after dark. But the boys would be there, a fire would be going, and a hot supper would be ready.

As for lunch, the man pressed his hand against the bulging bundle under his jacket. The bundle was also tucked under his shirt, wrapped in a handkerchief against his skin. It was the only way to keep the biscuits from freezing. He smiled happily as he thought of them, soaking in bacon grease and each with a big slice of fried bacon inside.

[3]A claim is a piece of public land that is staked out by a miner, settler, etc.

He plunged in among the big spruce trees. The trail was faint. A foot of snow had fallen since the last sled had passed over. He was glad he traveled light, without a sled. In fact, he carried nothing but the lunch wrapped in the handkerchief.

He was surprised, however, at the cold. It certainly was cold, he decided, as he rubbed his numb nose and cheeks with his mittened hand. He was a warm-whiskered man. But the hair on his face did not protect his cheeks or his nose that stuck out into the frosty air.

At the man's heels trotted a dog. It was a big, grey-coated husky. It had been born and bred here. In appearance and temper, it did not seem any different from its brother, the wild wolf.

The animal was depressed by the tremendous cold. It knew it was no time for traveling. Its **instinct** was more accurate than the man's judgment.

In reality, it was not merely colder than fifty below zero. It was colder than sixty below, than seventy below. It was seventy-five below zero. Since the freezing point is thirty-two above zero, it meant that there was one hundred and seven degrees of frost.

The dog did not know anything about thermometers. Possibly its brain could not even grasp the temperature as the man's could. But the brute had its instinct. A vague and alarming fear quieted it and made it slink along at the man's heels. This fear caused it to question every unusual movement the man made. It seemed as though the dog was expecting the man to reach camp or to seek shelter somewhere and build a fire.

The dog had learned fire, and it wanted fire. If not that, it wanted to **burrow** under the snow and bury its warmth away from the air.

The dog's moist breath had frozen and settled on its fur

in a fine powder of frost. Its jaws, snout, and eyelashes were especially whitened by its frozen breath.

The man's red beard and mustache were frosted, too, but more solidly. The frost took the form of ice and increased with every warm, moist breath he breathed out.

Also, the man was chewing tobacco. The ice held his lips so tightly that he was not able to clear his chin to spit the juice. The result was that a yellow beard made out of ice was increasing its length on his chin.

If he fell down, the icicle would shatter like glass into brittle pieces. But he didn't much mind the new addition. It was the penalty all tobacco chewers paid in that country. And he had been out before in two cold spells. They had not been as cold as this, he knew. But he recalled that the thermometer at Sixty Mile had read fifty below and fifty-five below.

He continued through the level stretch of woods for several miles. After crossing a flat area of stumps, he dropped down to a frozen stream bed. This was Henderson Creek, and he knew he was ten miles from the forks.

He looked at his watch. It was ten o'clock. He was making four miles an hour. He figured he would arrive at the forks at half-past twelve. He decided to celebrate that event by eating his lunch there.

The dog dropped in again at his heels. With a drooping tail showing his unhappiness, he followed the man along the creek bed. The channel of the old sled trail was plainly visible. But a dozen inches of snow covered any marks left by the last sled. No man had come up or down that silent creek in a month.

The man continued steadily. He did not usually think much. Just then, he had nothing to think about except eating lunch at the forks and being in camp with the boys at six o'clock. There was nobody to talk to. Anyway, it would have been impossible to talk because of the ice around his mouth. So he continued to chew tobacco and to increase the length of his yellow beard.

Once in a while the thought came back to him that it was very cold and that he had never felt such cold. As he walked along, he rubbed his cheeks and nose with the back of his mittened hand. He did this **automatically**. Now and again he changed hands.

But rub as he would, the instant he stopped, his cheeks went numb. The next instant the end of his nose went numb. He knew he was sure to frost his cheeks.

The man felt a stab of regret that he had not made a nose strap of the sort Bud wore in cold spells. Such a strap passed across the cheeks, as well, and saved them.

But it didn't matter much, after all. What were frostbitten cheeks? A bit painful, that was all. They were never serious.

Even though the man wasn't thinking, he was very **observant**. He noticed the changes in the creek, the curves and bends, and the jammed timber. Always he sharply noted where he placed his feet. Coming around a bend once, he backed away suddenly, like a startled horse. Then he curved away from his path and retreated several paces.

He knew the creek was frozen clear to the bottom. In this arctic winter, no creek could contain water. But he also knew there were springs that bubbled out from the hillsides. The springs ran along under the snow and on top of the ice on the creek. Even the coldest spells never froze these springs.

He also knew their dangers. They were traps. They hid pools of water under the snow that might be three inches or three feet deep.

Sometimes a skin of ice half an inch thick covered the springs. In turn, this was covered by snow. Sometimes there were alternate layers of water and ice skin. Therefore, when one broke through, one kept on breaking through each layer for a while. Sometimes a person would get soaked to the waist.

That was why the man had backed away in such panic. He had felt the hidden ice give under his feet and had heard the crackle. And to get his feet wet at this temperature meant trouble and danger.

At the very least it would hold him up. He would be forced to stop and build a fire. Then with the fire's protection, he would have to bare his feet while he dried his socks and moccasins.

The man stood and studied the creek bed and its banks. He decided the flow of water came from the right. The man thought for a while, rubbing his nose and cheeks. Then he moved to the left, stepping carefully and testing the footing for each step. Once clear of the danger, he took a fresh chew of tobacco and swung along at his four-mile pace.

During the next two hours, he came upon several similar traps. Usually the snow above the hidden pools had a sunken, cotton candy appearance that would warn him.

However, he once again had a close call. And once when the man suspected danger, he forced the dog to go in front. The dog did not want to go. It hung back until the man shoved it forward. Then it went quickly across the white, unbroken surface.

Suddenly the dog broke through the snow-covered ice. It **floundered** to one side and got to firmer footing.

Its front paws and legs had gotten wet. Almost immediately the water began to turn to ice. The dog made quick efforts to lick the ice off its legs. Then it dropped down in the snow and began to bite out the ice that had formed between its toes.

This was a matter of instinct. If the ice were not removed, the dog's feet would be sore. But the dog did not know this. It merely obeyed some mysterious urge deep within its nature.

However, the man knew about ice and sore feet. He took off a mitten and helped tear out the bits of ice from the dog's paws.

He did not **expose** his fingers more than a minute, so he was astonished at the numbness that quickly struck them. It certainly was cold. He pulled on the mitten quickly and beat his hand savagely across his chest.

At twelve o'clock the day was at its brightest. Yet the sun was too far south on its winter journey to show over the horizon. The bulge of the earth stood between the sun and Henderson Creek. So though the man was walking under a clear sky at noon, he cast no shadow.

At half-past twelve to the minute, he arrived at the forks of the creek. He was pleased at the speed he had made. If he kept it up, he would certainly be with the boys by six.

The man unbuttoned his jacket and shirt and took out his lunch. It took him no more than fifteen seconds. Yet in that brief moment, the numbness gripped his exposed fingers.

He did not put the mitten on. Instead, he struck his fingers sharply against his leg. Then he sat down on a snow-covered log to eat.

The stinging of his fingers stopped so quickly that he was startled. He had had no chance to take a bite of biscuit. He struck the fingers again and again and returned them to the mitten. Then he took off his other mitten so he could eat with his left hand.

The man tried to take a mouthful, but the ice beard prevented it. He had forgotten to build a fire and thaw out.

He chuckled at his foolishness. Even as he chuckled, he noted the numbness creeping into the exposed fingers. Also, he noted that the stinging his toes had felt when he first sat down was already gone.

He wondered whether the toes were warm or numb. He

moved them inside the moccasins and decided that they were numb.

He pulled the mitten on hurriedly and stood up. He was a bit frightened. He stamped up and down until the stinging returned to his feet.

It certainly was cold, was his thought. That man from Sulphur Creek had spoken the truth when telling how cold it got in the country. And he had laughed at him at the time! That showed one must not be too sure of things.

There was no mistake about it, it was cold. He paced up and down, stamping his feet and flapping his arms until calmed by the returning warmth. Then he got out matches and began to make a fire.

He got his firewood from the underbrush, where he found a supply of burnable twigs. Working carefully from a small beginning, he soon had a roaring fire. He thawed the ice from his face. Then he ate his biscuits in the fire's warmth. For the moment the cold was outsmarted.

The dog took satisfaction in the fire. It stretched out close enough for warmth and far enough away to escape being burned.

When the man had finished, he filled his pipe and took his time smoking it. Then he pulled on his mittens, set the ear flaps firmly over his ears, and took the creek trail up the left fork.

The dog was disappointed and **yearned** back toward the fire. This man did not know cold. Possibly all the man's ancestors had been ignorant of cold. Perhaps they did not know about real cold—cold one hundred and seven degrees below freezing point.

But the dog knew. All its ancestors knew, and it had inherited the knowledge. And it knew that it was not good to travel in such fearful cold. It was the time to lie snug in a hole in the snow, waiting for the cold to pass.

On the other hand, there was no great friendship between

the dog and the man. The one was the slave of the other. The only strokes it had ever received were the strokes of a whiplash and the frightening shouts that warned of a whiplash.

So the dog made no effort to communicate its fears to the man. It was not concerned for the man's **welfare**. It was for its own sake that it yearned to go back to the fire. But the man whistled and spoke to the dog with the sound of whiplashes. The dog swung in at the man's heels and followed.

The man took a chew of tobacco and began a new yellow icicle. Also, his moist breath quickly powdered his mustache, eyebrows, and lashes with white. There did not seem to be so many springs on the left fork of the Henderson. For half an hour the man saw no signs of any.

And then it happened. It happened at a place where there were no signs, where the soft, unbroken snow looked like solid ground underneath. There the man broke through.

It was not deep. But the man was wet halfway to the knees before he floundered out to firm ground.

He was angry and cursed his luck aloud. He had hoped to reach camp at six o'clock. This would delay him an hour. Now he would have to build a fire and dry out his footgear. He must do this at the low temperature—he knew that much.

He turned aside to the bank, which he climbed. On top, tangled in the underbrush near some spruces, was a bunch of dry firewood. It was mostly sticks and twigs. But there were also larger branches and dry grasses from last year.

The man threw down several large pieces on top of the snow. This served as the **foundation**. This base would keep the little flame from drowning in the snow it would melt.

He got the flame by touching a match to a small shred of birch bark that he took from his pocket. This burned even more easily than paper. Placing it on the foundation, he fed the little flame with grass and the tiniest dry twigs.

He worked slowly and carefully, strongly aware of his danger. As the flame grew, he gradually increased the size of the twigs he fed it. He squatted in the snow, pulling the twigs out from the brush and feeding them directly to the flame.

The man knew there must be no failure. When it is seventy-five below zero, a man must not fail in his first attempt to build a fire—that is, if his feet are wet. If his feet are dry and he fails, he can run along the trail. After half a mile, he can get the feeling back into them.

But in wet and freezing feet, feeling cannot be restored by running when it is seventy-five below. No matter how fast he runs, the wet feet will freeze the harder.

All this the man knew. The old-timer on Sulphur Creek had told him about it the **previous** fall. Now he was grateful for the advice. Already all **sensation** had gone out of his feet. To build the fire, he had to remove his mittens. His fingers had quickly gone numb.

His pace of four miles an hour had kept the blood pumping to the surface of his body, his toes, and fingers. But the instant he stopped, his heart had stopped pumping so hard.

The cold of space struck the unprotected tip of the planet. Since he was on that unprotected tip, he was hit by the full force of that blow. The blood in his body drew back from it. The blood was alive, like the dog. And like the dog, it wanted to hide away and cover itself up from the fearful cold.

So long as he walked four miles an hour, he pumped that blood to the surface. Now it retreated and sank deep down into his body.

His feet and fingers were the first to feel this absence of blood. His wet feet froze the faster and his fingers grew numb the faster. However, they had not yet begun to freeze.

Nose and cheeks were already freezing. Meanwhile, his skin chilled as it lost its blood.

But he was safe. Toes and nose and cheeks would only be touched by the frost. At last the fire was beginning to burn with strength. He was feeding it with twigs the size of his finger.

In another minute he would be able to feed it with branches the size of his wrist. Then he could take off his wet footgear. While it dried, he could keep his naked feet warm by the fire. He would rub them at first with snow, of course.

The fire was a success. He was safe. He remembered the advice of the old-timer at Sulphur Creek and smiled. The old-timer had been very serious in declaring that no man must travel alone in the Klondike after fifty below.

Well, here he was. He had had the accident. He was alone, and he had saved himself.

Some of those old-timers were rather womanish, he thought. All a man had to do was keep his head and he would be all right. Any man who was a man could travel alone.

But it was surprising how rapidly his cheeks and nose were freezing. And he had not thought his fingers could go lifeless in so short a time. But they were lifeless. He could barely make them move together to grip a twig. They seemed far away from his body and from him. When he touched a twig, he had to look and see if he had hold of it. The links between him and his fingers were pretty well broken.

All of that did not matter much. There was the fire. It snapped and crackled and promised life with each dancing flame.

He started to untie his moccasins. They were coated with ice. The thick German socks felt like iron coatings clamped around his lower legs. The moccasin strings were like rods of steel. They were all twisted and knotted as if by a fire.

For a moment he tugged with his numb fingers. Then he realized it was impossible, and he drew his knife.

But before he could cut the strings, it happened. It was his own fault, or rather his mistake. He should not have built the fire under the spruce tree. He should have built it in the open. But it had been easier to pull the twigs from the brush and drop them directly on the fire.

Now the tree under which he had done this carried a weight of snow on its branches. No wind had blown for weeks. Now each branch was fully loaded. Each time he had pulled a twig, he had slightly disturbed the tree.

This disturbance was invisible to the man. But it was **sufficient** to bring about the disaster. High up in the tree, one branch dropped its load of snow. This snow fell on the branches beneath it, causing them to drop their load.

This process continued. It spread out and involved the whole tree. It grew like an avalanche, and the snow fell without warning on the man and the fire.

The fire was wiped out! Where it had burned was a covering of fresh and disordered snow.

The man was shocked. It was as though he had just heard his own death sentence. For a moment he sat and stared at the spot where the fire had been.

Then he grew very calm. Perhaps the old-timer at Sulphur Creek was right. If he had only had a traveling partner, he would have been in no danger now. His partner could have built the fire.

Well, it was up to him to build the fire over again. This second time there must be no failure. Even if he succeeded, he would most likely lose some toes. His feet must be badly frozen by now. And there would be some time before the second fire was ready.

These were his thoughts, but he did not sit and think them. He was busy all the time they were passing through his mind.

He made a new foundation for a fire, this time in the open. There no tree could wipe it out.

Next he gathered dry grasses and tiny twigs from piles left by the river. He could not bring his fingers together to pull them out, but he could gather them by the handful. In this way he got many rotten twigs and bits of green moss which he did not want. But this was the best he could do.

He worked in an orderly way. He even collected an armful of larger branches to be used when the fire gathered strength.

And all the while the dog sat and watched him. There was a certain yearning longing in its eyes. He looked upon the man as the fire provider, and the fire was slow in coming.

When all was ready, the man reached in his pocket for a second piece of birch bark. He knew the bark was there. Though he could not feel it with his fingers, he could hear its crisp rustling as he fumbled for it. But no matter how he tried, he could not clutch hold of it.

All this time, he was aware that each instant his feet were freezing. This thought tended to put him in a panic. But he fought against it and kept calm. He pulled on his mittens with his teeth. Then he flapped his arms back and forth. He beat his hands against his sides with all his might. He did this sitting down, and he stood up to do it.

All the while, the dog sat in the snow. Its wolflike tail was curled warmly over its front feet. Its sharp wolf ears bent forward **intently** as it watched the man. And the man felt a great gush of envy of this creature who was warm and secure in its natural covering.

After a time the man was aware of the first faraway signs of sensation in his fingers. The faint tingling grew stronger. It became a stinging ache that was terribly painful. But the man welcomed the pain with satisfaction.

He stripped the mitten from his right hand and pulled

out the birch bark. The exposed fingers were quickly going numb again. Next he brought out his bunch of matches.

But the tremendous cold had already driven the life out of his fingers. In his effort to separate one match from the others, the whole bunch fell in the snow. He tried to pick them out of the snow, but failed. The dead fingers could neither touch nor clutch.

He was very careful. He drove the thought of his freezing feet, nose, and cheeks out of his mind. He **devoted** his whole soul to the matches. He watched, using his vision instead of his touch.

When he saw his fingers on each side of the bunch, he closed them. That is, he tried to close them. But the links between his brain and fingers were broken, and his fingers did not obey.

He pulled the mitten on the right hand and beat it fiercely against his knee. Then, with both hands, he scooped the bunch of matches—along with much snow—into his lap. Yet he was no better off.

After a few tries, he managed to get the bunch between the heels of his mittened hands. In this way he carried it to his mouth. The ice crackled and snapped when he opened his mouth with a violent effort.

He pushed his lower jaw back and curled his upper lip out of the way. Then he scraped the bunch of matches with his upper teeth in order to separate a match.

He succeeded in getting one, which he dropped on his lap. He was no better off. He could not pick it up.

Then he **devised** a way. He picked the match up in his teeth and scratched it on his leg. Twenty times he scratched before he succeeded in lighting it.

As it flamed, he held it with his teeth to the birch bark. But the burning smoke went up his nose and into his lungs, and he coughed. The match fell into the snow and went out.

The old-timer on Sulphur Creek was right, he thought

with controlled hopelessness. After fifty below, a man should travel with a partner.

He beat his hands but failed to waken any sensation in them. Suddenly he took off both mittens with his teeth. He grabbed the whole bunch of matches between the heels of his hands. Since his arm muscles were not frozen, he was able to press the heels of his hands tightly against the matches. Then he scratched the bunch along his leg.

It flared into flame, seventy matches at once! There was no wind to blow them out.

Keeping his head away from the strangling smoke, he held the blazing matches to the birch bark. As he held it, he became aware of sensation in his hand. His flesh was burning. He could smell it. Deep down below the surface he could feel it.

The sensation developed into sharp pain. And still he endured it. He held the matches clumsily to the bark that would not light because his own burning hands were in the way.

At last when he could endure no more, he jerked his hands apart. The blazing matches fell sizzling into the snow. But the birch bark was alight. He began laying dry grasses and the tiniest twigs on the flame.

He could not pick and choose because he had to lift the fuel with the heels of his hands. Small pieces of rotten wood and green moss stuck to the twigs. He bit them off as well as he could with his teeth.

He protected the flame carefully and awkwardly. It meant life, and it must not die.

The disappearance of blood from the surface of his body now made him begin to shiver. He grew more awkward. A large piece of green moss fell directly on the little fire. He tried to poke it out with his fingers. But his shivering body made him poke too far. He disturbed the **nucleus** of the little fire. The burning grasses and tiny twigs separated and scattered.

He tried to poke them together again. But in spite of his tense effort, his shivering caused him to scatter the twigs beyond all hope. Each twig gushed a puff of smoke and went out.

The fire provider had failed. As he looked unemotionally about him, he happened to observe the dog. It was sitting in the snow across the ruins of the fire from him. It was moving restlessly and hunching its body. First it lifted one front leg, then the other. It shifted its weight back and forth with longing eagerness.

The sight of the dog put a wild idea into the man's head. He remembered the tale of a man who was caught in a blizzard. He had killed a steer and crawled inside the dead body. The plan had saved him.

The man decided he would kill the dog. He could then bury his hands in the warm body until the numbness went out of them. After that, he could build another fire.

He spoke to the dog, calling it to him. But in his voice was a strange note of fear that frightened the animal. The dog had never known the man to speak in such a way before.

Something was the matter. Its suspicious nature sensed danger. It didn't know what danger. But for some reason, it feared the man.

It flattened its ears down at the sound of the man's voice. Its shifting became more restless, but it would not come to the man.

The man got on his hands and knees and crawled toward the dog. This unusual posture made the dog even more suspicious. It edged away sideways from the man.

The man sat up in the snow for a moment and struggled for calmness. Then he pulled on his mittens with his teeth and got to his feet. He glanced down at first in order to make sure that he was really standing up. The absence of sensation in his feet left him unrelated to the earth.

The fact that the man was now standing started to drive

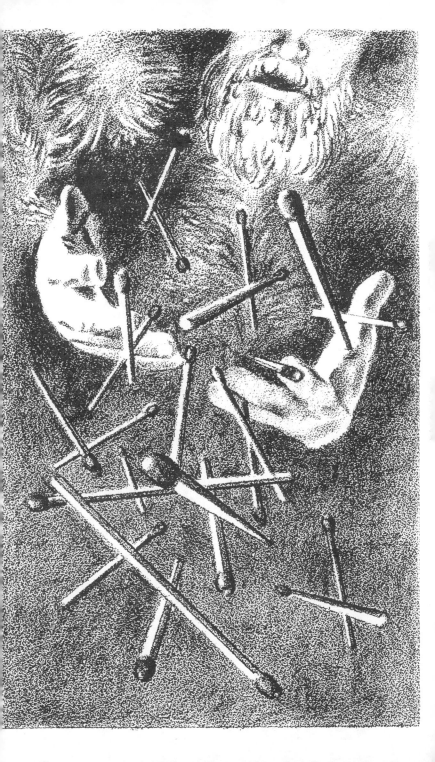

the suspicion from the dog's mind. And when the man spoke with the sound of whiplashes, the dog obeyed as usual and came to him.

As it came within reach, the man lost control. His arms flashed out to the dog. He felt **genuine** surprise to find his hands could not clutch. His fingers could not bend or feel either. He had forgotten for the moment that they were frozen and that they were freezing more and more.

All this happened quickly. Before the animal could get away, he circled his arms around its body. He sat down in the snow and held the dog while it snarled and whined and struggled.

But that was all the man could do—hold its body and sit there. He realized that he could not kill the dog. There was no way to do it. With his helpless hands, he could not draw or hold his knife or strangle the animal.

He released it. It charged wildly away, its tail between its legs and still snarling. It halted forty feet away. There it watched the man curiously with ears sharply bent forward.

The man looked down at his hands in order to locate them. He found them hanging on the end of his arms. It struck him as curious that one should have to use his eyes to find his hands.

He began flapping his arms back and forth, beating the mittened hands against his sides. He did this for five minutes, violently. His heart pumped enough blood to the surface to stop his shivering.

But there was still no sensation in his hands. He had the impression that they hung like weights on the ends of his arms. But when he tried to trace that impression, he could not find it.

A fear of death, dull and heavy, came to him. This fear quickly became sharp as he realized it was not just a matter of freezing his fingers or toes. It was not even merely the possibility of losing his hands and feet. It was now a matter of life and death, with the chances against him.

This threw him into a panic. He turned and ran up the creek bed along the old, dim trail. The dog joined in behind and kept up with him. The man ran blindly, without purpose. He ran in fear such as he had never known in his life.

Slowly, as he plowed and floundered through the snow, he began to see things again. He took in the banks of the creek, the old timber jams, the leafless aspens, and the sky.

The running made him feel better. He did not shiver. Maybe, if he ran on, his feet would thaw out. Anyway, if he ran far enough, he would reach camp and the boys.

Without doubt he would lose some fingers and toes and some of his face. But the boys would take care of him. They would save the rest of him when he got there.

At the same time another thought in his mind said he would never get to camp. It was too many miles away. The freezing had too great a start on him. He would soon be stiff and dead.

This thought he kept in the back of his mind and refused to consider. Sometimes it pushed itself forward and demanded to be heard. But he pushed it back and tried to think of other things.

It struck him as curious that he could run at all on feet so frozen that he could not feel them when they struck the earth. He seemed to skim along above the surface and to have no connection with the earth. Somewhere he had once seen a winged Mercury.[4] He wondered if Mercury felt as he felt when skimming over the earth.

His idea of running until he reached camp and the boys had one flaw. He lacked the strength. Several times he stumbled. Finally he swayed, crumpled up, and fell. When he tried to rise, he failed. He must sit and rest, he decided. Next time he would merely walk and keep going.

[4]Mercury was a god of the ancient Romans. He delivered messages for other gods and wore winged sandals.

As he sat and got his breath back, he noted that he felt quite warm and comfortable. He was not shivering. It even seemed that a warm glow had come to his body.

And yet, when he touched his nose or cheeks, there was no sensation. Running would not thaw them out. Nor would it thaw out his hands and feet.

Then it came to him that more and more parts of his body must be freezing. He tried to ignore this thought, to forget it, to think of something else. He was aware of the panicky feeling it caused, and he was afraid of the panic.

But the thought pushed forward and stayed with him. Finally it gave him the vision of his body totally frozen.

This was too much. He made another wild run along the trail. Once he slowed down to a walk. But the thought of the freezing spreading itself made him run again.

And all the time the dog ran with him, at his heels. When the man fell down a second time, it curled its tail over its front feet and sat facing him. It had a curiously eager and intent look.

The warmth and security of the animal angered the man. He cursed the dog till it flattened its ears in a begging way.

This time the shivering came more quickly upon the man. He was losing in his battle with the frost. It was creeping into his body from all sides. The thought of it drove him on. But he ran no more than a hundred feet when he staggered and fell headfirst.

It was his last panic. He got back his breath and control. Then he sat up and began to think about meeting death with dignity.

However, this idea did not come to him in terms like that. His thought was that he had been making a fool of himself, running around like a chicken with its head cut off. That was the comparison that came to his mind.

Well, he was bound to freeze anyway. He might as well take it properly.

With this new peace of mind came the first hints of drowsiness. A good idea, he thought, to sleep off to death.

It was like taking an anesthetic.[5] Freezing was not so bad as people thought. There were lots worse ways to die.

He pictured the boys finding his body the next day. Suddenly he found himself with them, coming along the trail and looking for himself. And, still with them, he came around a turn in the trail. There he found himself lying in the snow.

He did not belong with himself anymore. Even then he was outside himself, standing with the boys and looking at himself in the snow.

It certainly was cold, was his thought. When he got back to the States, he could tell the folks what real cold was.

He drifted on from this to a picture of the old-timer on Sulphur Creek. He could see him quite clearly, warm and comfortable, and smoking a pipe.

"You were right, old fella; you were right," the man mumbled to the old-timer of Sulphur Creek.

Then the man dozed off into what seemed to him the most comfortable and satisfying sleep he had ever known.

The dog sat facing him and waiting. The brief day drew to a close in a long, slow twilight. There were no signs of a fire to be made. Never had the dog known a man to sit like that in the snow and make no fire.

As the twilight drew on, its eager yearning for the fire overpowered it. Lifting and shifting its front feet, it whined softly. Then it flattened its ears down, waiting to be scolded by the man. But the man remained silent.

Later the dog whined loudly. And still later it crept close to the man and caught the scent of death. This made the animal bristle and back away.

A little longer it delayed, howling under the stars that leaped and danced and shone brightly in the cold sky. Then it turned and trotted up the trail in the direction of the camp it knew. There it would find the other food providers and fire providers.

[5]An anesthetic is a drug that numbs feeling and pain.

"To Build a Fire" was first published in 1910.

INSIGHTS INTO
JACK LONDON

(1876-1916)

London began work as a child to help support his family. First, he was a newspaper boy. Then he got a job at a cannery. There he sometimes worked up to twenty hours a day. At age 16, he became an oyster pirate. After that he turned patrolman, then became a sailor and went to Japan. London also shoveled coal, but he soon quit. He learned he was doing the work of two men while being paid less than either one. Finally, London grew tired of all these jobs and became a hobo.

London had little time for schooling. But he claimed he often read up to nineteen hours a day. He tried to get more formal education. He went back to school at an academy in order to enter the university. But the academy kicked him out. The school feared its reputation would be hurt because London was doing two years of work in one semester.

London went to the Klondike in 1897 to hunt for gold. He didn't strike it rich. In fact, all he found was fool's gold. But London did find a gold mine in one sense. The stories he heard around the campfires would later become material for his writing.

London firmly set out to become a writer. He wrote steadily, 1,000 words a day, six days a week. Often he had to mail out a story many times because it was rejected again and again. But London was a careful bookkeeper. He kept track of how much it cost him to mail out each story. When the stamps cost more than the fee he could expect for a story, he stopped sending the story out.

London's struggle for success as a writer was not a painless one. Friends recall seeing a five-foot high stack of rejection slips hanging from a hook in his bedroom.

In sixteen years, Jack London wrote fifty books. By the time he died, he was probably the most famous and best-paid writer in the world. He earned over a million dollars for his work.

At times, scholars have criticized London's writing. Yet he has always been popular with the public. His books and stories have been translated into nearly sixty different languages. Over forty movies based on his work have been made.

Other works by London:
  The Call of the Wild, novel
  The Sea Wolf, novel
  White Fang, novel

THE RANSOM
OF RED CHIEF

O. HENRY

VOCABULARY PREVIEW

Below is a list of words that appear in the story. Read the list and get to know the words before you start the story.

aimlessly—without aim or purpose
anxiously—with worry and fear
captive—prisoner
chronic—lasting a long time
desperate—reckless and daring
egotism—the habit of being too self-centered or proud of oneself
ferocious—fierce and cruel
graft—bribes or money dishonestly taken
imp—child who enjoys making mischief
impudent—rude and sassy
martyrs—people who die heroically for their beliefs
porous—filled with small openings
prominent—leading or well known
proposition—a proposed or suggested scheme
provisions—supplies, especially food and drink
rowdy—rough and noisy
spendthrift—one who foolishly and wastefully spends money
sullenly—in a gloomy and sulky way
terrorized—frightened and filled with terror
treachery—an act that betrays a person, group, or country; disloyalty

THE RANSOM OF RED CHIEF

O. HENRY

Sam and Bill are two sharp con men. They need just a little more money to pull off their biggest con. So they decide to kidnap a wild ten-year-old boy and hold him for ransom. The ransom finally gets paid, but not quite according to Sam and Bill's scheme.

It looked like a good thing: but wait till I tell you. We were down South, in Alabama—Bill Driscoll and myself—when we thought of this kidnapping idea. It was "during an instant of momentary madness," as Bill said afterward. But we didn't find that out till later.

There was a town down there as flat as a pancake. It was called Summit,[1] of course. The people who lived there were as harmless and happy a group of peasants as ever gathered around a Maypole.

[1] A summit is a high point in an area. Sam is being sarcastic.

Bill and me had about six hundred dollars between us. We needed just two thousand dollars more to pull off a dishonest land scheme in western Illinois.

We talked it over on the front steps of the hotel. Parents' love for their children, says we, is strong in little towns. So a kidnapping job should do better there than in areas where reporters are sent out to stir up talk.

We knew that Summit couldn't come after us with anything stronger than the police and maybe some lazy bloodhounds. And maybe they'd write an angry line or two in the *Weekly Farmer's Budget*. So, it looked good.

We chose for our victim the only child of a **prominent** citizen named Ebenezer Dorset. The father was respectable and tight with his money. He was a mortgage buyer; a stern, honest passer of collection plates; and a forecloser.[2]

The kid was a freckle-faced boy of ten with freckles that stood out. His hair was the color of the cover of the magazine you buy at the newsstand when you want to catch a train.

Bill and me figured that we could shake down Ebenezer for a ransom of two thousand dollars to the last cent. But wait till I tell you.

About two miles from Summit was a little mountain covered with a thick growth of cedars. At the back of the mountain near the top was a cave. There we stored **provisions**.

One evening after sundown, we drove in a buggy past old Dorset's house. The kid was in the street. He was throwing rocks at a kitten on a fence.

"Hey, little boy!" says Bill, "would you like to have a bag of candy and a nice ride?"

The boy hits Bill square in the eye with a piece of brick.

"That will cost the old man an extra five hundred dollars," says Bill, climbing over the wheel.

That boy put up a fight like a boxing bear. At last we

[2]A mortgage is a deed that gives someone a claim to property in case a debt is not repaid. To foreclose is to take over a piece of property when a debt is not repaid.

got him down in the bottom of the buggy and drove away. We took him up to the cave. Then I hitched the horse in the cedars.

After dark I drove the buggy three miles to the little village where we had rented it. Then I walked back to the mountain.

Bill was putting bandages over the scratches and bruises on his face. There was a fire burning behind the big rock at the entrance of the cave. The boy was watching a pot of boiling coffee. He had two buzzard tail feathers stuck in his red hair.

He points a stick at me when I come up and says, "Ha, damned paleface! Do you dare to enter the camp of Red Chief, the terror of the plains?"

"He's all right now," says Bill. He rolled up his pants and looked at the bruises on his legs.

"We're playing Indian. We're making Buffalo Bill's show seem as exciting as a town meeting.[3] I'm Old Hank, the Trapper, Red Chief's **captive**. I'm to be scalped at daybreak. By Geronimo, that kid can kick hard!"

Yes, sir, that boy seemed to be having the time of his life. The fun of camping out in a cave had made him forget that he was a captive himself. He named me Snake-eye, the Spy. He told me when his braves returned from the warpath, I was to be broiled at the stake at dawn.

Then we had supper. He filled his mouth full of bacon and bread and gravy. At the same time, he began to talk. He made a speech during dinner that went something like this:

"I like this fine. I never camped out before. But I had a pet 'possom once, and I was nine on my last birthday. I hate to go to school. Rats ate up sixteen of Jimmy Talbot's aunt's speckled hen's eggs. Are there any real Indians in these woods? I want some more gravy. Does the trees moving make the wind blow? We had five puppies. What makes your nose so red, Hank? My father has lots of money. Are

[3]Bill means that their play is so wild that it tops Buffalo Bill's Wild West Show.

the stars hot? I whipped Ed Walker twice on Saturday. I don't like girls. You'd better not catch toads unless you use a string. Do oxen make any noise? Why are oranges round? Have you got beds to sleep on in this cave? Amos Murray has got six toes. A parrot can talk, but a monkey or a fish can't. How many does it take to make twelve?"

Every few minutes he would remember that he was a pesky redskin. Then he'd pick up his stick rifle and tiptoe to the mouth of the cave. There he'd look for the scouts of the hated paleface.

Now and then he would let out a war whoop that made Old Hank the Trapper shake. That boy had Bill **terrorized** from the start.

"Red Chief," says I to the kid, "would you like to go home?"

"Aw, what for?" says he. "I don't have any fun at home. I hate to go to school. I like to camp out. You won't take me back home again, Snake-eye, will you?"

"Not right away," says I. "We'll stay here in the cave awhile."

"All right!" says he. "That'll be fine. I never had such fun in all my life."

We went to bed about eleven o'clock. We spread down some wide blankets and quilts and put Red Chief between us. We weren't afraid he'd run away. He kept us awake for three hours, jumping up and reaching for his rifle. "Listen, partner!" he screeched in my ears and Bill's. He did this whenever he imagined that the crackle of a twig or the rustle of a leaf meant that outlaws were sneaking up.

At last I fell into a restless sleep. I dreamed that I had been kidnapped and chained to a tree by a **ferocious** pirate with red hair.

Just at daybreak, I was awakened by several awful screams from Bill. They weren't yells, or howls, or shouts, such as you'd expect from a man. They were like the screams of women when they see ghosts or caterpillars. It's an awful thing to hear a strong, **desperate**, fat man scream without any control in a cave at daybreak.

I jumped up to see what the matter was. Red Chief was sitting on Bill's chest, with one hand tangled in Bill's hair. In the other he had the sharp knife we used for slicing bacon. He was trying very hard and with great realism to scalp Bill. That was the sentence that Bill had been given the evening before.

I got the knife away from the kid and made him lie down again. But, from that moment, Bill's spirit was broken. He lay down on his side of the bed. But he never closed an eye again to sleep as long as that boy was with us.

I dozed off for a while. But close to sunup, I remembered that Red Chief had said I was to be burned at the stake at dawn. I wasn't nervous or afraid. But I sat up and lit my pipe and leaned against a rock.

"What are you getting up so soon for, Sam?" asked Bill.

"Me?" says I. "Oh, I got a kind of a pain in my shoulder. I thought sitting up would rest it."

"You're a liar!" says Bill. "You're afraid. You was to be burned at sunrise, and you was afraid he'd do it. And he would, too, if he could find a match.

"Ain't it awful, Sam? Do you think anybody will pay out money to get a little **imp** like that back home?"

"Sure," said I. "A **rowdy** kid like that is just the kind that parents love. Now, you and the Chief get up and cook breakfast. I'll go up on the top of this mountain and scout around."

I went up on the peak of the little mountain and ran my eye over the area. Over toward Summit I expected to see the village folk. I thought they would be armed with scythes[4] and pitchforks, searching the countryside for the kidnappers.

[4]Scythes are tools with curved blades used for cutting grass or grain.

But what I saw was a peaceful landscape and one man plowing with a mule. Nobody was searching the creek. No messengers dashed back and forth to tell the worried parents that there was no news. Instead, there was a sleepiness throughout that part of Alabama that lay before my eyes.

"Perhaps," says I to myself, "they haven't yet found out that the wolves have taken the little lamb from the flock. Heaven help the wolves!" says I. And I went down the mountain to breakfast.

When I got to the cave, I found Bill backed up against the side of it, breathing hard. The boy looked as though he was ready to smash him with a rock half as big as a coconut.

"He put a red-hot boiled potato down my back," explained Bill. "Then he mashed it with his foot. I smacked his ears. Have you got a gun with you, Sam?"

I took the rock away from the boy and kind of patched up the argument.

"I'll fix you," says the kid to Bill. "No man ever yet hit Red Chief who didn't get paid back. You better beware!"

After breakfast the kid takes something out of his pocket. It was a piece of leather with strings wrapped around it. He goes outside the cave unwinding it.

"What's he up to now?" says Bill, **anxiously**. "You don't think he'll run away, do you, Sam?"

"No fear of it," says I. "He don't seem to be much of a stay-at-home type. But we've got to fix up some plan about the ransom.

"There don't seem to be much excitement around Summit because he's disappeared. Maybe they haven't realized yet that he's gone. His folks may think he's spending the night with Aunt Jane or one of the neighbors.

"Anyhow, he'll be missed today. Tonight we must get a message to his father demanding the two thousand dollars for his return."

Just then we heard a kind of war whoop. David might have shouted like this when he knocked out the champion Goliath. It was a sling that Red Chief had pulled out of his pocket. Now he was whirling it around his head.

I dodged and heard a heavy thud and a kind of sigh from Bill. A horse makes the same sound when you take his saddle off. A rock the size of an egg had hit Bill just behind his left ear.

Bill went limp. Then he fell in the fire across the frying pan of hot dishwater. I dragged him out and poured cold water on his head for half an hour.

After a while, Bill sits up and feels behind his ear. He says, "Sam, do you know who my favorite Biblical character is?"

"Take it easy," says I. "You'll come to your senses shortly."

"King Herod,"[5] says he. "You won't go away and leave me here alone, will you, Sam?"

I went out and caught that boy. I shook him until his freckles rattled.

"If you don't behave," says I, "I'll take you straight home. Now, are you going to be good or not?"

"I was only playing a joke," says he **sullenly**. "I didn't mean to hurt Old Hank. But what did he hit me for? I'll behave, Snake-eye, if you won't send me home. And if you'll let me play the Black Scout today."

"I don't know the game," says I. "That's for you and Mr. Bill to decide. He's your playmate for the day. I'm going away for a while on business.

"Now, you come in and make friends with him. Say you're sorry for hurting him. If you don't, you'll go home at once."

I made him and Bill shake hands. Then I took Bill aside and told him I was going to Poplar Cove. Poplar Cove was a little village three miles from the cave. I wanted to find

[5]The Bible says that King Herod (73?-4 B.C.) ordered all the children of Bethlehem to be murdered.

out there what Summit was saying about the kidnapping.

Also, I thought it best to send a stern letter to old man Dorset that day. I was going to demand the ransom and order how it should be paid.

"You know, Sam," says Bill, "I've stood by you. Without blinking an eye, I faced earthquakes, fire, and flood. I stuck with you in poker games, dynamite explosions, police raids, train robberies, and cyclones.

"I never lost my nerve yet till we kidnapped that two-legged rocket of a kid. He's got me going. You won't leave me long with him, will you, Sam?"

"I'll be back sometime this afternoon," says I. "You must keep the boy amused and quiet till I return. And now we'll write the letter to old Dorset."

Bill and I got paper and pencil and worked on the letter. Meanwhile, Red Chief strutted up and down with a blanket wrapped around him. He was guarding the mouth of the cave. Bill begged me tearfully to make the ransom fifteen hundred dollars instead of two thousand.

"I ain't trying," says he, "to say anything against the well-known love of parents for their kids.

"But we're dealing with humans. It ain't human for anybody to give up two thousand dollars for that forty-pound chunk of freckled wildcat.

"I'm willing to take a chance asking fifteen hundred dollars. I'll even pay the difference."

So, to relieve Bill, I agreed. Together we wrote a letter that ran this way:

EBENEZER DORSET, ESQ.:[6]
We have your boy hidden in a place far from Summit. It is useless for you or even the best detectives to try to find him. Absolutely the only terms on which you can have him back are these:

---

[6]Esq. is an abbreviation for Esquire. This is a title of respect for a man which is placed after his last name.

We demand fifteen hundred dollars in large bills for his return. The money is to be left at midnight tonight at the same spot and in the same box as your reply—as described below.

If you agree to these terms, send your answer in writing by a lone messenger tonight at half-past eight o'clock. Take the road to Poplar Cove and cross Owl Creek. There you'll see three large trees about a hundred yards apart. They are close to the fence of the wheat field on the right-hand side. Go to the bottom of the fence post across from the third tree. You will find a small cardboard box.

The messenger will place the answer in this box and return immediately to Summit.

If you try any **treachery** *or do not meet the demands in this letter, you will never see your boy again.*

If you pay the money as demanded, he will be returned to you safe and well within three hours. These terms are final. If you do not agree to them, we won't try to reach you again.

TWO DESPERATE MEN

I addressed this letter to Dorset. Then I put it in my pocket. As I was about to start, the kid comes up to me and says, "Aw, Snake-eye, you said I could play the Black Scout while you was gone."

"Play it, of course," says I. "Mr. Bill will play with you. What kind of a game is it?"

"I'm the Black Scout," says Red Chief. "I have to ride to the fort to warn the settlers that the Indians are coming. I'm tired of playing Indian myself. I want to be the Black Scout."

"All right," says I. "It sounds harmless to me. I guess Mr. Bill will help you outsmart the pesky Indians."

"What am I supposed to do?" says Bill, looking at the kid with suspicion.

"You are the horse," says Black Scout. "Get down on your hands and knees. How can I ride to the fort without a horse?"

"You'd better keep him interested," said I, "till we get the scheme going. Loosen up."

Bill gets down on his all fours. A look comes in his eye like a rabbit's when you catch it in a trap.

"How far is it to the fort, kid?" he asks in a hoarse voice.

"Ninety miles," says the Black Scout. "And you have to move it to get there on time. Whoa, now!"

The Black Scout jumps on Bill's back. Then he digs his heels in Bill's side.

"For heaven's sake," says Bill, "hurry back, Sam, as soon as you can. I wish we hadn't made the ransom more than a thousand. Say, you quit kicking me, or I'll get up and spank you good."

I walked over to Poplar Cove and sat around the post office and store. I talked with the hicks that came in to buy something. One bearded fellow says that he hears Summit is all upset because Old Ebenezer Dorset's boy was lost or stolen.

That was all I wanted to know. I bought some smoking tobacco and casually mentioned the price of black-eyed peas. Then I mailed my letter secretly and walked away. The postmaster said the mailman would come by in an hour to take the mail to Summit.

When I got back to the cave, Bill and the boy weren't there. I searched around the cave and risked a shout or two, but there was no response.

So I lighted my pipe and sat down on a mossy bank to wait for something to happen.

In about half an hour, I heard the bushes rustle. Bill wobbled out into the little clearing in front of the cave. Behind him was the kid. He came stepping softly like a scout, with a broad grin on his face.

Bill stopped, took off his hat, and wiped his face with a red handkerchief. The kid stopped about eight feet behind him.

"Sam," says Bill, "I suppose you'll think I'm a traitor. But I couldn't help it. I'm a grown person with a man's ways and habits of defending myself. But there is a time when all types of **egotism** and control fail.

"The boy is gone. I have sent him home. All our plans are off.

"There was **martyrs** in old times," goes on Bill. "They died rather than give up the kind of **graft** they enjoyed. None of 'em ever was forced to suffer such inhuman tortures as I have. I tried to be faithful to our laws of pirating. But there came a limit."

"What's the trouble, Bill?" I ask him.

"I was rode," says Bill, "the ninety miles to the fort, not one inch less. Then, when the settlers was rescued, I was given oats. Sand ain't a tasty substitute.

"Then for an hour I tried to explain to him why there was nothin' in holes. And I also tried to tell him how a road can run both ways and what makes the grass green.

"I tell you, Sam, a human can only stand so much. I takes him by the neck of his clothes and drags him down the mountain. On the way he kicks my legs black and blue from the knees down. And I've got to have two or three bites on my hand treated.

"But he's gone," continues Bill, "gone home. I showed him the road to Summit. I also kicked him about eight feet nearer there at one kick.

"I'm sorry we lose the ransom. But it was either that or send Bill Driscoll to the madhouse."

Bill is puffing and blowing. But there is a look of peace and growing contentment on his rosy face that can't be described.

"Bill," says I, "there isn't any heart disease in your family, is there?"

"No," says Bill. "Nothing **chronic** except malaria[7] and accidents. Why?"

"Then you might turn around," says I, "and have a look behind you."

Bill turns and sees the boy. He grows pale and sits down hard on the ground. He begins to pick at grass and little sticks **aimlessly**.

For an hour I was afraid he'd gone crazy. And I told him that my scheme was to finish up the whole job at once. We would get the ransom and be off with it by midnight if old Dorset agreed to our **proposition**.

So Bill got up enough courage to give the kid a weak smile. And he promised to play the Russian in a Japanese war with him when he felt better.

I had a scheme for getting that ransom without being trapped by opposing plots. Professional kidnappers should find it interesting. The tree under which the answer and the money were to be left was close to the road fence. There were big, bare fields on all sides. If a gang of police officers should be watching for anyone to come for the note, they could see him from a long way off.

But no, sirree! At half-past eight, I was up in that tree. I was as well hidden as a tree toad, waiting for the messenger to arrive.

Right on time, a half-grown boy rides up the road on a bicycle. He locates the cardboard box at the foot of the fence post. Then he slips a folded piece of paper into it. After that he pedals back toward Summit.

I waited an hour and then decided no one was going to play any tricks. I slid down the tree and got the note. Then I slipped along the fence till I reached the woods. I was back at the cave in another half an hour.

[7]Malaria is a disease carried by mosquitoes which causes fevers that recur.

I opened the note, got near the lantern, and read it to Bill. It was written with a pen in poor handwriting. The sum and total of it was this:

TWO DESPERATE MEN
GENTLEMEN: I received your letter today about the ransom for the return of my son. I think your demands are a little high. So I am now making you a proposition which I believe you will accept.

You bring Johnny home and pay me two hundred and fifty dollars in cash. I will then agree to take him off your hands.

You had better come at night, for the neighbors believe he is lost. I couldn't be responsible for what they would do to anybody they saw bringing him back.

Very respectfully,
EBENEZER DORSET

"Great pirates of Penzance!"[8] says I; "of all the **impudent**—"

But I glanced at Bill and hesitated. He had the most pleading look I ever saw on the face of a speechless or a talking animal.

"Sam," says he, "what's two hundred and fifty dollars, after all? We've got the money. One more night of this kid will send me to a bed in the madhouse.

"Besides being a true gentleman, I think Mr. Dorset is a **spendthrift** for making us such a generous offer. You ain't going to pass up the chance, are you?"

"To tell you the truth, Bill," says I, "this little lamb has got on my nerves a bit, too. We'll take him home and pay the ransom. Then we'll make our getaway."

We took him home that night. We got him to go by telling him that his father had bought a rifle and a pair of moccasins

[8]The pirates of Penzance are in a comic opera by Gilbert and Sullivan.

for him. We also said we were going to hunt bears the next day.

It was just twelve o'clock when we knocked at Ebenezer's front door. Right at the moment, I should have been taking the fifteen hundred dollars from the box under the tree. Instead, Bill was counting out two hundred and fifty dollars into Dorset's hand.

When the kid found out we were going to leave him at home, he started to howl like a pipe organ. He grabbed Bill's leg as tight as a leech. His father peeled him away bit by bit, like a **porous** plaster.

"How long can you hold him?" asks Bill.

"I'm not as strong as I used to be," says old Dorset. "But I think I can promise you ten minutes."

"Enough," says Bill. "In ten minutes I shall cross the central, southern, and middle western states and be heading for Canada."

It was dark, and Bill was fat, and I'm a good runner. But he was a good mile and a half out of Summit before I could catch up with him.

"The Ransom of Red Chief" was first published in 1910.

INSIGHTS INTO
O. HENRY

(1862-1910)

O. Henry's real name was William Sydney Porter. He adopted his pen name and began writing stories while in prison.

Before O. Henry was sent to prison, he fled the country to try to escape the law. He went to Honduras where he met the outlaws Al and Frank Jennings. The Jennings brothers had just robbed a Texas bank of $30,000. O. Henry helped them spend the loot. But he refused their offer to join in another robbery.

When O. Henry returned to the U.S., he was found guilty of taking money from a bank where he had worked. He served three years in prison for this crime.

O. Henry was a crack shot. According to one prison worker, he was also a powerful fighter. Once O. Henry saw a huge prisoner threaten the prison doctor. O. Henry leaped over a counter, knocked the prisoner out with one blow, and returned to his job. The amazed doctor said, "He did not utter a word."

O. Henry often completely "wrote" out his stories in his mind. He could tell them perfectly to a listener. But putting the stories down on paper was another matter. He would hesitate and fret, writing it out at a very slow pace.

The Saturday Evening Post once sent O. Henry a check for $1,000 as payment. All the famous magazine asked in return was a piece of "anything" he had written. The *Post* added they would be happy to pay more. But O. Henry recalled that the *Post* had turned down some of his best pieces when he was younger. He mailed the check back without any explanation.

Other works by O. Henry:
"The Cop and the Anthem," short story
"The Furnished Room," short story
"The Gift of the Magi," short story
"A Municipal Report," short story
"A Retrieved Reformation," short story

RIP VAN WINKLE

WASHINGTON IRVING

VOCABULARY PREVIEW

Below is a list of words that appear in the story. Read the list and get to know the words before you start the story.

awe—feeling of respect mixed with fear and amazement
bustling—moving quickly and with great energy
decay—to rot or fall apart
despotism—government by a ruler with total power who is usually cruel; tyranny
faltering—hesitating or stuttering
guardian—one who watches over and defends; protector
henpecked—constantly nagged and ordered about by a wife
keener—sharper
lapse—passage of a certain amount of time
listlessly—showing no energy or enthusiasm
majestic—grand and noble
persecution—constant cruel and unfair treatment
preceding—coming before
profitable—bringing gains or benefits
provoked—produced; caused a reaction
refugee—a person fleeing danger and seeking a safe place to live
shrew—scolding, hot-tempered woman
stout—thick, heavy, and solidly built
tottered—walked with a wobble
tyranny—government by a ruler with total power who is usually cruel; despotism

RIP VAN WINKLE

WASHINGTON IRVING

Rip Van Winkle is a kind man, adored by all. Only his wife scolds him for being lazy.

To find peace from her nagging, Rip goes hunting in the mountains. But magic leads him astray and into an amazing adventure.

Anyone who has ever traveled up the Hudson River remembers the Catskill Mountains. They are a branch of the Appalachian mountain range and rise on the west side of the river. They swell up to a grand height and seem to rule over the countryside.

The color and shape of the mountains change with the seasons and the weather. They even change with the hour. All the wives, far and near, think the Catskills are perfect for forecasting the weather. When the weather is fair and calm, the mountains look blue and purple. Then their bold outlines stand out against the clear evening sky.

But sometimes grey clouds gather on top of the mountains, even when the rest of the sky is cloudless. At sunset those clouds will glow and light up like a crown of glory.

A village lies at the foot of these magical mountains. It can be spotted just where the blue of the hills fades into the fresh green of the landscape. The traveler may have seen the light smoke curling up from this town with its gleaming shingle roofs.

It is a little village and very old. Dutch colonists built it in the early days of the region. That was at the time that good Peter Stuyvesant[1] (may he rest in peace!) had just become governor.

Within a few years, the original settlers had built houses out of small yellow bricks from Holland. These houses had decorative windows and gables. Many homes were topped by weathervanes.

Many years ago, when the country was still ruled by Great Britain, a man named Rip Van Winkle lived in this village. Rip lived in one of those yellow brick houses. But to tell the truth, it was sadly run-down and weather-beaten.

Rip was descended from the Van Winkles who had bravely fought for Peter Stuyvesant. These Van Winkles had even gone with Stuyvesant to the fight at Fort Christina.

However, Rip had inherited few warlike traits from his ancestors. He was just a simple, good-natured man. Moreover, he was a kind neighbor and an obedient, **henpecked** husband.

The fact that he was henpecked might explain why he showed that patience which made him so popular. Men are

---

[1]Peter Stuyvesant (1610?-1672) was the last Dutch governor of New Netherland. New Netherland included land in present-day New York and several nearby states.

most likely to be agreeable around town when they are ruled by **shrews** at home. Without a doubt, the fiery furnace of troubles at home makes their tempers flexible. Some lectures are worth all the sermons in the world for teaching patience.

Therefore, a shrewish wife may be considered a blessing in some ways. If so, Rip was blessed three times over.

It is certainly true that he was a great favorite among all the women of the village. As members of the friendly sex usually do, they took his side in family quarrels. And when they chatted in the evenings, they would blame Mrs. Van Winkle.

The children of the village, too, would shout for joy whenever Rip approached. He joined in their games and made their toys. He also taught them to fly kites and shoot marbles. He told them long stories, too, about ghosts, witches, and Indians.

Whenever Rip went dodging about the village, he was surrounded by a troop of children. They would hang onto his coattails and climb on his back. Those children would play a thousand tricks on Rip without fear of being punished. And in all these chases, not one dog would bark at Rip.

The great fault in Rip's character was a dislike for any kind of **profitable** job. It's not that he wasn't hardworking or determined. He could fish all day, sitting on a wet rock with a pole as long and heavy as a lance. He wouldn't even complain if he didn't get a single nibble. He would carry a gun through woods and swamps, up and down hills, to shoot a few squirrels or pigeons.

And Rip never refused to help a neighbor even with the roughest chore. He was always the first man to arrive when corn was husked or stone fences were built.

The women of the village asked him to run errands, too. He would even do chores their less willing husbands would not do.

In short, Rip was ready to attend to anybody's business but his own. As for doing his duty to his family and keeping his farm in order—he found that impossible.

In fact, Rip said it was no use to work on his farm. He said it was the most rotten piece of ground in the whole country. Everything about it went wrong and would go wrong, in spite of him.

For example, his fences were continually falling to pieces. And his cow would either wander off or get into the cabbages. Weeds were sure to grow quicker in his fields than anywhere else. The rain always made a point of beginning just as he had some outdoor work to do.

The land Rip had inherited slipped away, acre by acre. Finally there was little more left than a patch of Indian corn and potatoes. Yet, despite the fact he had less to care for, Rip had the most run-down farm in the neighborhood.

His children, too, were as ragged and wild as if they did not have parents. His son Rip looked just like his father.

Young Rip seemed to have inherited his father's habits along with his old clothes. He was generally seen trotting along like a colt at his mother's heels. He wore a pair of his father's old trousers. He was always struggling to hold up these pants with one hand. He looked like a lady holding the bottom of her long dress.

Rip Van Winkle was one of those happy people of foolish, contented character. Such types take the world easy. They eat white bread or brown—whichever is the least trouble to get. They would rather starve on a penny than work for a pound.[2] Left to himself, Rip would have whistled his life away, perfectly content.

But Rip's wife kept scolding about his laziness, carelessness, and the ruin he was bringing on his family. Her tongue was always going—morning, noon, and night. Everything he said or did was sure to bring about a rush of household speeches.

[2]A pound is a British sum of money.

Rip had just one way to reply to all lectures of this kind. He would shrug his shoulders, shake his head, and roll his eyes. But he never said anything.

However, this always **provoked** a fresh speech from his wife. Rip would be forced to retreat from the house and go outside. That side is the only side which really belongs to a henpecked husband.

Rip's only supporter at home was his dog, Wolf. Wolf was just as henpecked as his master. Mrs. Van Winkle thought they were companions in their idle ways. She even glared at Wolf because she thought he often caused his master to go wrong.

It is true that Wolf was as brave an animal as ever hunted the woods. But what courage could stand up to the endless and total terrors of a woman's tongue?

The moment Wolf entered the house, his head fell and his tail drooped or curled between his legs. He sneaked along with a guilty look, glancing at Mrs. Van Winkle out of the corner of his eye. If he saw a broom or dipper move, he would fly to the door yelping.

Times grew worse and worse for Rip Van Winkle as years of marriage rolled by. A bitter tongue never grows smoother with age. And a sharp tongue is the only tool with an edge that gets **keener** with constant use.

For a long while, Rip used to cheer himself by visiting a kind of ongoing club. This club was made up of wisemen, thinkers, and other idle people in the village. The club held its meetings on a bench in front of a small inn where a rosy picture of King George III[3] hung.

Here the men of the club used to sit in the shade during a long, lazy summer's day. They would talk **listlessly** over village gossip or tell endless sleepy stories about nothing.

But it was a different story when some traveler passed by and left behind an old newspaper. Then any politician would have gladly paid to have heard their deep discussions.

---

[3]King George III, who ruled England from 1760-1820, was king during the American Revolution.

The club members would seriously listen to Derrick Van Bummel slowly read out the paper's contents.

Van Bummel, the schoolmaster, was a neat, learned little man. He was not frightened by even the biggest word in the dictionary.

After listening to the news, the club would wisely debate the events which had taken place much earlier. But the opinions of this group were completely controlled by Nicholas Vedder.

Vedder was a leader of the village and landlord of the inn. He would sit at the door of the inn from morning till night. He would move only enough to avoid the sun and keep in the shade of a large tree. The neighbors could tell what time it was by his position as accurately as with a sundial.

It is true that Vedder was rarely heard to speak. Instead, he smoked his pipe without stopping.

But his supporters (for every great man has his supporters) understood him perfectly. They knew how to gather his opinions. When he heard anything that displeased him, he was seen to smoke his pipe furiously. Then he would send out short, frequent, and angry puffs.

But when Vedder was pleased, he would inhale the smoke slowly and calmly. Light and peaceful clouds would drift from the pipe. Sometimes Vedder would even take the pipe from his mouth. The sweet-smelling smoke would curl around his nose. Then he would nod his head seriously as a sign of his complete approval.

The unlucky Rip was chased from even this stronghold by his shrewish wife. She would suddenly break in upon the peaceful gathering and criticize all the members. Even that grand person, Nicholas Vedder, was not safe from the daring tongue of this terrible shrew. She charged him with encouraging her husband to be idle.

Poor Rip at last became almost hopeless. His only way to escape from farmwork and his wife's noise was to take his gun and stroll into the woods. Here he would sometimes sit at the foot of a tree and share a meal with Wolf. Rip felt sympathy for the dog as another creature who suffered **persecution**.

"Poor Wolf," he would say. "The lady of the house makes you lead a dog's life. But never mind, my lad. While I live, you shall never lack for a friend to stand by you!"

On hearing this, Wolf would wag his tail and look sadly into his master's face. If dogs can feel pity, I truly believe he felt as his master did with all his heart.

One fine autumn day, Rip went on a long stroll. Without thinking, he scrambled to one of the highest parts of the Catskills. He was hunting squirrels, his favorite sport. The still, lonely places echoed and re-echoed with his gunshots.

Late that afternoon, Rip reached a green hill. The little hill, covered with mountain herbs, stood at the top of a cliff. There Rip sat down, panting and tired.

From an opening between the trees, Rip could see all the rich woodland below. At a distance he saw the great Hudson River. Far, far below him it moved on its silent but **majestic** path. Here and there a purple cloud or the sail of a slow ship was reflected on its glassy surface. At last the river wound away, losing itself in the blue hills.

On the other side Rip could see a mountain glen.[4] It was a wild, lonely, and rough place. The bottom was filled with rocks from overhanging cliffs. It was scarcely lighted by the reflected rays of the sun.

For some time Rip lay thinking about this scene. Evening was gradually coming. The mountains began to throw their long blue shadows over the valley. He saw that it would be dark long before he could reach the village. He gave a heavy sigh when he thought of facing the terrors of Mrs. Van Winkle.

---

[4]A glen is a narrow valley.

As he was about to start down, he heard a voice from a distance. "Rip Van Winkle! Rip Van Winkle!" it called.

Rip looked round. But he saw nothing but a crow flying alone across the mountain.

Rip thought his imagination must have tricked him. He turned to start down again. But then he heard the same cry ring through the still evening air. "Rip Van Winkle! Rip Van Winkle!"

At the same time, Wolf's hair rose, and he gave a low growl. He crept to his master's side and looked fearfully down into the glen.

Rip now felt a vague fear creep over him. He looked anxiously in the same direction. Then he saw a strange figure slowly climbing up the rocks. This person was bending under the weight of something he carried on his back.

Rip was surprised to see any human being in this lonely and out-of-the-way place. But thinking that the man was a neighbor in need of help, he hurried down to give it.

When he got closer, Rip was still more surprised at how unusual the stranger looked. He was a short, squarely built old fellow. He had thick, bushy hair and a gray beard.

The stranger's dress was in the old Dutch style. He wore a sleeveless jacket strapped around his waist and several pair of knickers. The outer pair was quite baggy. Rows of buttons ran down the side.

This old fellow carried a heavy keg on his shoulder. It seemed to be full of liquor. He gestured for Rip to come near and help him with the load.

Rip was rather shy and did not trust this new friend. However, he obeyed the fellow with his usual speed. Rip took the keg, and the fellow took Rip's gun. Then they climbed up a narrow gully. It was apparently the dry bed of a mountain stream.

As they climbed, Rip heard every now and then long rolling rumbles like distant thunder. These sounds seemed to come from a deep ravine or opening. This opening lay right between two high rocks on the rugged path.

Rip paused for an instant. But he guessed that it was one of those passing storms that occur in the mountains. So he decided to go on.

They passed through the ravine and reached a small valley. This valley looked like a small arena. Tall cliffs surrounded it. At the edges of those cliffs, tree branches hung down. The branches partly blocked the view of the blue sky and the bright evening clouds.

During their whole trip, Rip and his companion had walked on in silence. Rip had greatly wondered what was the point of carrying a keg up this wild mountain. Yet there was something strange and puzzling about the unknown. This filled him with **awe** and kept him from being too friendly.

On entering the arena, more strange sights were seen. On a flat spot in the center was a company of odd-looking people playing ninepins.[5]

These people were dressed in an old-fashioned, odd style. Some wore doublets.[6] Others wore short jackets and carried long knives in their belts. Most had baggy knickers like Rip's guide.

Their faces, too, were peculiar. One had a full beard, broad face, and small piggish eyes. Another one had a huge nose and wore a white hat decorated with a red rooster's tail. They all had beards, of various shapes and colors.

There was one who seemed to be the commander. He was a **stout** old gentleman with a weather-beaten face. He wore a laced doublet and a broad belt with a short sword. He also had a hat and feather, red stockings, and high-heeled shoes decorated with roses made out of ribbons.

The whole group reminded Rip of the characters in an old Flemish painting he had seen. The painting had been brought over from Holland when the village was first settled.

[5]Ninepins is a game like bowling.

[6]A doublet is a man's roomy jacket with or without sleeves.

Now it hung in the parlor of Pastor Van Shaick, the village parson.

What seemed odd to Rip was that these folks were apparently playing a game. Yet their faces were serious, and they remained mysteriously silent.

Altogether, they were the saddest group of merrymakers that Rip had ever seen. Nothing broke the stillness of the scene but the noise of the balls. Whenever they rolled, these balls echoed along the mountains like thunder.

As Rip and his companion approached, the group suddenly stopped playing. They stared at Rip with a statue-like look and strange, rude, dull faces. The sight made Rip's heart turn inside of him and his knees shake.

His companion now emptied the contents of the keg into bottles. Then he motioned for Rip to serve the group. Rip obeyed with fear and trembling. The men drank the liquor in deep silence. Then they returned to their game.

Little by little, Rip's awe and fear faded. He even dared to taste the drink when no one was looking at him. He thought it had much the same flavor as an excellent gin from Holland.

Rip was by nature a thirsty person. He was soon tempted to try another drink. One taste provoked another. Finally he had gone back to the cup so often that his senses were overpowered. His eyes swam and his head gradually drooped. Soon he fell into a deep sleep.

When he awoke, Rip found himself on the hill where he had first seen the old man. He rubbed his eyes—it was a bright sunny morning. The birds were hopping and twittering among the bushes. He saw an eagle circling overhead and flying through the pure mountain breeze.

"Surely," Rip thought, "I have not slept here all night."

He recalled what happened before he fell asleep. The strange man with a keg of liquor. The mountain ravine. The

wild place among the rocks. The sad group playing ninepins. And the cup—

"Oh, that cup! That wicked cup!" thought Rip. "What excuse can I give Mrs. Van Winkle?"

He looked around for his gun. But, instead of his clean, well-oiled gun, he found an old, rusty firearm. The barrel was crusted with rust, the trigger had fallen off, and the handle was worm-eaten. He now suspected that the grim partygoers of the mountain had followed him. After having given him the liquor, they had robbed him of his gun.

Wolf, too, had disappeared. But Rip thought he might have strayed away after a squirrel or partridge. Rip whistled for him and shouted his name but without result. The echoes repeated his whistle and shout. But no dog appeared.

Rip decided to revisit the scene of the last evening's party. If he met anyone from that group, he intended to demand his gun and dog.

As Rip got up to walk, he found his joints were stiff. He also felt unusually tired.

"These mountain beds do not agree with me," thought Rip. "If that little party gave me rheumatism,[7] Mrs. Van Winkle will give me a terrible time."

With some trouble, Rip got down into the glen. He found the gully which he and his companion had climbed the **preceding** evening. But to his astonishment, a mountain stream was now foaming down it. The stream leapt from rock to rock and filled the glen with babbling murmurs.

Rip managed to scramble up the side of the stream. Then he worked his way through clumps of birch, sassafras, and witch hazel. Sometimes the wild grapevines that ran from tree to tree tripped or tangled Rip's feet.

At last Rip reached the spot where the ravine had led to the arena. But there was no opening now. The cliffs were high and could not be scaled. And a waterfall came tumbling over those rocks in a sheet of feathery foam. The water fell

---

[7]Rheumatism is a disease that causes muscles or joints to be stiff and sore.

into a broad deep pool. This pool was black from the shadows of the surrounding forest.

Here, then, poor Rip was forced to stop. He again called and whistled for his dog. He was only answered by the cawing of crows who darted about a dry tree on a sunny cliff. Feeling safe at that height, they seemed to be laughing at the poor man's confusion.

As he approached the village, Rip met a number of people. But he did not know any of them. This surprised him somewhat. He had thought he knew everyone in the area. They also were dressed in a different style from what he was used to.

The strangers all stared at Rip with equal signs of surprise. Whenever they looked at him, they always stroked their chins. After seeing them make this gesture so often, Rip did the same thing without thinking. Then he realized to his astonishment that his beard had grown a foot long!

Rip now entered the outskirts of the village. A troop of strange children ran at his heels. They laughed at him and pointed at his gray beard. The dogs too were all unfamiliar to Rip. They barked at him as he passed.

The village itself was changed. It was larger and more people lived there now. There were rows of houses he had never seen before. Those which he had known well had disappeared. Strange names were over the doors. Strange faces were at the windows. Everything was strange.

Rip now had serious doubts. He began to wonder if he and the world around him were bewitched. Surely this was his native village which he had left the day before.

There stood the Catskills. And there was the silver Hudson in the distance. There was every hill and valley exactly as it had always been.

Rip was deeply puzzled. "That cup last night," he thought, "has sadly confused my poor head!"

Rip had some trouble finding the way to his own house.

He approached it silently with awe. He expected to hear the high-pitched voice of Mrs. Van Winkle.

Instead, he found the house had begun to **decay**. The roof had fallen in, windows were shattered, and the doors were off the hinges.

A half-starved dog that looked like Wolf was lurking about. Rip called him by name. But the dog snarled, showed his teeth, and went on. This was an unkind insult, indeed.

"Even my dog," poor Rip sighed, "has forgotten me."

Rip entered the house which Mrs. Van Winkle had always kept in neat order. Now it was empty, lonely, and apparently abandoned.

This emptiness overcame all the fears Rip had as a married man. He called loudly for his wife and children. His voice echoed in the lonely rooms for a moment. Then all was silent again.

Rip now hurried out of the house and hastily went to his old hideaway, the village inn.

But it too was gone. A large, rickety wooden building stood in its place. It had huge open windows. Some of them were broken but had been mended with old hats and petticoats. A sign, "The Union Hotel, by Jonathan Doolittle," was painted over the door.

The great tree was gone that used to shelter the quiet little Dutch inn. Now a tall, bare pole stood there. On top of it was something that looked like a red nightcap.[8] From it fluttered a flag which was covered with an odd design of stars and stripes. All this was strange and unfamiliar.

However, Rip did recognize the picture on the sign. He had peacefully smoked his pipe under this picture many times. It was the rosy face of King George.

But even this was strangely changed. Instead of a red coat, the man in the picture wore a blue and tan coat.[9] Instead of a scepter,[10] he held a sword in his hand. On his head he

[8]This pole and cap were symbols of liberty during the Revolution.

[9]These were the colors of the Revolutionary Army.

[10]A scepter is a staff that symbolizes royal power.

wore a three-cornered hat. Underneath the picture was painted in large letters, GENERAL WASHINGTON.

As usual, there was a crowd of people around the door. But there was no one that Rip recognized. Even the character of the people seemed changed. There was a busy, **bustling**, quarreling mood to the crowd. The usual lack of interest and sleepy calm was gone.

Rip looked for the wise Nicholas Vedder with his broad face, double chin, and long pipe. He should be there spouting clouds of smoke instead of pointless speeches.

Rip also looked for Van Bummel, the schoolmaster. He should be there reading out the contents of an old newspaper. But they were not there.

In place of these, there was a lean, mean-looking fellow with his pockets full of fliers. He was furiously raving about rights, elections, members of Congress, freedom, Bunker Hill,[11] the heroes of seventy-six. These and other words were nonsense to the bewildered Van Winkle.

Rip's appearance soon attracted the attention of the people talking politics at the inn. They crowded around him with great curiosity, eyeing him from head to foot. They looked at his long gray beard, his rusty gun, his strange clothing. Then they stared at the army of women and children at his heels.

The man who had been giving the speech hurried up to Rip. Drawing Rip away from the crowd, he asked, "Which side do you vote for?" Rip stared at him in empty-headed stupidity.

Then another short but busy little fellow pulled him by the arm. Raising up on tiptoe, he asked in his ear, "Are you a Federal or a Democrat?"[12] Rip was just as much at a loss in understanding that question.

Then a knowing, self-important old man in a pointed, three-cornered hat made his way through the crowd. He pushed the people with his elbows as he passed. He planted

[11]Bunker Hill is the site of a famous battle of the Revolution.

[12]These were two political parties in early U.S. history.

himself in front of Van Winkle, with one hand on his hip and the other on his cane. His sharp eyes and pointed hat almost seemed to pierce Rip's soul.

He demanded in a stern voice, "What brings you to the election with a gun and a mob at your heels? Do you mean to start a riot in the village?"

"Alas! Gentlemen," cried Rip, "I am a poor, quiet man. I was born in this village. And I am a loyal subject of the king, God bless him!"

A shout burst from the crowd. "A British lover! A British lover! A spy! A **refugee**! Get him out of here! Away with him!"

The man in the three-cornered hat had some trouble restoring order. He frowned with a look of great sternness. And he demanded again, "Why have you come here? Whom are you seeking?"

Poor Rip humbly swore that he meant no harm. He was simply searching for some of his old neighbors who used to sit around the inn.

"Well, who are they? Name them," the man said.

Rip thought a moment. Then he asked, "Where's Nicholas Vedder?"

There was silence for a little while. Then an old man replied in a thin, high voice, "Nicholas Vedder! Why, he's been dead and gone for the past eighteen years! There was a wooden marker in the churchyard that used to tell all about him. But that's rotten and gone, too."

"Where's Brom Dutcher?" Rip asked.

"Oh, he went off to the army at the beginning of the war. Some say he was killed at the storming of Stony Point.[13] Others say he drowned in a storm at the foot of Antony's Nose.[14] I don't know. He never came back again."

"Where's Van Bummel, the schoolmaster?"

"He went off to the wars, too. He was a great general and is now in Congress."

---

[13]Stony Point was the site of a battle during the American Revolution.

[14]Antony's Nose is a mountain on the Hudson River.

Rip was heartbroken about these sad changes in his home and friends and at finding himself alone in the world. Every answer he heard puzzled him, too. He could not understand such huge **lapses** of time and matters such as war, Congress, and Stony Point.

Rip had no courage to ask about any more friends. But he cried out in despair, "Doesn't anyone here know Rip Van Winkle?"

"Oh, Rip Van Winkle!" exclaimed two or three. "Oh, sure! That's Rip Van Winkle over there, leaning against the tree."

Rip looked and saw an exact copy of himself as he had looked when he went up the mountain. The man pointed out was apparently just as lazy and certainly as ragged.

Poor Rip was now completely confused. He doubted his own identity. He wondered whether he was himself or another man.

In the middle of his bewilderment, the man in the three-cornered hat demanded, "Who are you? And what is your name?"

"God knows," Rip exclaimed, at his wit's end. "I'm not myself. I'm somebody else. That's me over there. No, that's somebody else in my shoes.

"I was myself last night, but I fell asleep on the mountain. They've changed my gun. And everything's changed. I'm changed. I can't tell what's my name or who I am!"

The people standing around now began to look at each other. They nodded and winked. Some tapped their fingers against their foreheads.

There also was a whisper about taking the old fellow's gun away to keep him from doing mischief. At hearing this suggested, the man in the three-cornered hat left quickly.

At this serious moment, a young, pretty woman pushed through the crowd. She wanted to get a peep at the gray-bearded man. She had a chubby child in her arms, which began to cry when he saw Rip.

"Hush, Rip," the woman said. "Hush, you little fool. The old man won't hurt you."

The name of the child, the woman's manner, and her tone of voice awakened memories in Rip's mind.

"What is your name, my good woman?" he asked.

"Judith Gardenier."

"And your father's name?"

"Ah, poor man," the woman said. "Rip Van Winkle was his name. But it's been twenty years since he took his gun and went away from home. And he has never been heard of since. His dog came home without him.

"But whether he shot himself, or was carried away by the Indians, nobody can tell. I was only a little girl then."

Rip had just one more question. In a **faltering** voice, he asked, "Where's your mother?"

"Oh, she too had died just a short time since," the woman said. "She broke a blood vessel in a fit of anger at a New England peddler."

There was a drop of comfort, at least, in this news. Honest Rip could not hold back any longer. He took his daughter and her child in his arms.

"I am your father!" he cried. "Young Rip Van Winkle once—old Rip Van Winkle now! Doesn't anybody know poor Rip Van Winkle?"

Everyone stood there amazed. Finally an old woman **tottered** out of the crowd. She put her hand to her brow and peered under it at Rip's face. After a moment, she exclaimed, "Sure enough! It is Rip Van Winkle. It is himself! Welcome home again, old neighbor. Why, where have you been these twenty long years?"

Rip's story was soon told. After all, the whole twenty years had been like just one night to him. The neighbors stared when they heard it. Some were seen to wink at each other and put their tongues in their cheeks.

The man in the three-cornered hat had returned after the scare was past. Now he turned down the corners of his mouth and shook his head. Following that, most of the group shook their heads.

They decided to ask the opinion of old Peter Vanderdonk, who was seen slowly walking up the road. Peter was a relative of a historian who wrote one of the first books about the area.

Peter was the oldest person in the village. And he knew all the wonderful events and traditions of the neighborhood. He remembered Rip at once and backed up his story completely.

Peter told the group that it was true that the Catskills were haunted by strange beings. That was a fact handed down from his ancestor, the historian.

It was also true that the great Hendrick Hudson appeared there every twenty years. Hudson had first discovered the river and nearby land. Those appearances of Hudson (along with his crew of the *Half-moon*) allowed him to revisit the places he explored. Like a **guardian**, he watched over the river and the great city called by his name.

Peter said that his father once saw Hudson and his crew. They were in their old Dutch clothing playing ninepins in a mountain valley. One summer afternoon Peter himself had heard the sound of the balls, rolling like distant thunder.

To make a long story short, the crowd broke up. They returned to the more important concerns of the election.

Rip's daughter took him home to live with her. She had a snug, well-furnished house. A stout, cheerful farmer was her husband. Rip remembered him as one of the children who used to climb on his back.

As to Rip's son, he was employed to work on the farm.

But young Rip had inherited his father's character in doing anything else but his own work.

Rip now returned to his old walks and habits. He soon found many of his old friends. However, they were all the worse for the wear and tear of time. Rip preferred to make new friends among the young people of the village. He soon became a great favorite with them.

Rip had nothing to do at home. He had arrived at that happy age when a man can be lazy without being blamed. So once more he took his place on the bench at the inn door. He became respected as a village leader and as a source of stories about the old times "before the war."

It was some time before Rip could follow the gossip or understand the strange events that had taken place while he slept. He learned how there had been a revolutionary war. And the country had thrown off the ties of old England. Now he was a free citizen of the United States, not a subject of his Majesty George the Third.

Rip was no politician. The changes of states and empires had little effect on him. But there was one kind of **despotism** under which he had groaned for a long time. That was government by petticoats.[15]

Fortunately, that was at an end. He had got his neck out of the bonds of marriage. Now he could go in and out when he pleased without dreading Mrs. Van Winkle's **tyranny**. Whenever her name was mentioned, he shook his head, shrugged, and rolled his eyes. This might be taken as a sign that he accepted his fate or was delighted by his freedom.

Rip used to tell his tale to every stranger who stayed at Mr. Doolittle's hotel. At first, he changed some points every time he told it. This was probably because he had so recently awakened.

At last he settled down to telling exactly the tale I have given. There wasn't a man, woman, or child in the village who didn't know it by heart.

---

[15]This means government by females, especially wives.

Some always pretended to doubt the truth of Rip's story. They insisted that Rip had been out of his head. They said Rip always remained a little crazy on this point.

But almost all of the old Dutch villagers believed the story completely. Even now when they hear a storm in the Catskills, they say that Hudson and his crew are playing ninepins.

And all henpecked husbands in the neighborhood have the same wish when they are weary. They long for just one soothing drink from Rip Van Winkle's cup.

"Rip Van Winkle" was first published in 1819.

INSIGHTS INTO WASHINGTON IRVING

(1783-1859)

Washington Irving was named after George Washington. Irving's nanny once introduced young Irving to President Washington. She told the President that Irving had been named after him. The President responded by patting Irving on the head and blessing him. Years later, Irving wrote four books about President Washington. This set of books was Irving's longest work.

One of Irving's first hits was the comical *History of New York*. As a joke, Irving pretended that a Dutchman named Diedrich Knickerbocker wrote the work. Critics liked the book. Even the illustrations were popular. Some pictures in the book showed Dutchmen in knee-length pants. Later, these pants came to be called "knickers" after Irving's phony author.

Irving never married. His sweetheart, Matilda Hoffman, died at the age of 17. After her death, Irving could not bear to hear her name mentioned. And he never forgot her. He kept Matilda's picture beside his bed for over fifty years, until he died in 1859.

Irving is best known for his American folk stories like "Rip Van Winkle" and "The Legend of Sleepy Hollow." But both these tales were really German folk tales. Irving simply rewrote the stories and gave them an American setting.

"Rip Van Winkle" has been called the world's most popular story. The tale was a hit on stage, too. One actor appeared in the play for forty-five years!

Other works by Irving:
   "The Devil and Tom Walker," short story
   "The Legend of Sleepy Hollow," short story

THE DEVIL AND DANIEL WEBSTER

STEPHEN VINCENT BENET

VOCABULARY PREVIEW

Below is a list of words that appear in the story. Read the list and get to know the words before you start the story.

abiding—accepting, obeying, or standing by

ambition—strong wish to get ahead or achieve something

compromise—a settlement where each side gives up something in order to agree

condemn—blame and criticize

distinct—clear; obvious

eloquence—polished, forceful speech

eternity—endless time, both past and future

fanatic—one who is filled with extreme, often dangerous enthusiasm for something

grimly—coldly and sternly

heir—one who receives property, position, etc., from a past owner

indivisible—not possible to break up

mockingly—in a way that pokes fun or sneers

patriarch—male leader of a family or tribe

pious—religious

pried—looked with curiosity; snooped

renegade—one who deserts a group, cause, etc., to join or believe in something else; defector

specimens—examples or types

transferred—moved

verdict—decision (especially by a jury)

wretch—unhappy or worthless person

The Devil and Daniel Webster

*Poor Jabez Stone makes a foolish bargain.
He sells his soul to a mysterious stranger
in exchange for ten years of good luck. Only
one man has a chance of delivering Jabez
from the clutches of the stranger — the
famous senator Daniel Webster.*

It's a story they tell in the border country—where Massachusetts joins Vermont and New Hampshire. Yes, Dan'l Webster's dead—or at least they buried him. But every time there's a thunderstorm around Marshfield, they say you can hear his rolling voice in the sky.

And they say if you go to his grave and speak loud and clear, "Dan'l Webster—Dan'l Webster!" the ground will begin to shiver. The trees will begin to shake. And after awhile,

Stephen Vincent Benet

a deep voice will ask, "Neighbor, how stands the Union?"[1]

Then you better answer, the Union stands as she stood. She's rock solid and covered in copper, one and **indivisible**. Otherwise, he might rise right up out of the ground. At least that's what I was told when I was a youngster.

You see, for a while Dan'l was the biggest man in the country. He never got to be president, but he was the biggest man. There were thousands that trusted him almost as much as God Almighty. They told stories about him and all the things that belonged to him. These stories were like the stories of **patriarchs** and such.

They said that when he stood up to speak, stars and stripes came right out in the sky. Once he spoke against a river and made it sink into the ground.

They said he'd take his fishing pole, Killall, to the woods. Then the trout would jump out of the streams right into his pockets. The fish knew it was no use putting up a fight against him.

They said, too, that when he argued a case, he could turn on the harps in heaven. He could even make the earth underground shake. That was the kind of man he was.

His big farm up at Marshfield suited him. The chickens he raised were all white meat down through the drumsticks. The cows were raised like children. The big ram he called Goliath had horns that curled like a morning-glory vine. Goliath could butt through an iron door.

But Dan'l wasn't one of your gentlemen farmers. He knew all the ways of the land. And he'd be up by candlelight to see that the chores got done. He had a mouth like a big dog, a forehead like a mountain, and eyes like burning coals. That was Dan'l Webster when he was younger.

The biggest case Dan'l ever argued never got written down in the books. That was because he argued it against the devil. It was nip and tuck and no holds barred. And this is the way I used to hear it told.

---

[1]The Union is another name for the United States.

There was a man named Jabez Stone, lived at Cross Corners, New Hampshire. He wasn't a bad man to start with, but he was an unlucky man. If he planted corn, he got insects. If he planted potatoes, he got blight.[2]

He had good-enough land, but it didn't make him rich. He had a good wife and children. But the more children he had, the less there was to feed them.

If stones appeared in his neighbor's field, boulders rose up in his. If he had a lame horse, he'd trade it in for a worse one and pay extra, too. There's some folks just born to be like that, I guess.

One day Jabez Stone got sick of the whole business. He'd been plowing that morning, and he'd just broke the plow on a rock. He could have sworn the rock hadn't been there yesterday.

As he stood looking at the plow, his horse began to cough. It was the kind of cough that means sickness and horse doctors. There were two children down with the measles and his wife was sick. He himself had an infected thumb. It was about the last straw for Jabez Stone.

"I swear," he said, looking around him hopelessly, "I swear it's enough to make a man want to sell his soul to the devil! And I would, too, for two cents!"

Then he felt a kind of strangeness come over him. He was worried a little about what he had said. But naturally he wouldn't take it back, being a New Hampshireman.

All the same, he felt relieved when evening came and nothing had happened, as far as he could see. He was a religious man, after all. But, just like the Bible says, someone always notices sooner or later.

And sure enough, a soft-spoken stranger in dark clothes showed up around suppertime the next day. He drove up in a handsome buggy and asked for Jabez Stone.

Well, Jabez told his family it was a lawyer, come to see him about a will. But he knew who it was. He didn't like

---

[2]Blight is a disease that ruins plants.

the looks of the stranger. And Jabez didn't like the way he smiled with his teeth. They were white teeth and there were many of them. Some say they were filed to a point. But I wouldn't swear to that.

Jabez Stone didn't like it either when his dog got a look at the stranger. The dog ran away howling with his tail between his legs.

But, having given his word more or less, Jabez stuck to it. They went out behind the barn and made their bargain. Jabez Stone had to prick his finger to sign. The stranger loaned him a silver pin. The wound healed clean. But it left a little white scar.

After that, all of a sudden things got better for Jabez Stone. His cows got fat and his horses sleek. His crops were the envy of the neighborhood. Lightning might strike all over in the valley, but it wouldn't strike his barn.

Pretty soon he was one of the richest people in the county. They asked him to run for town councilman, and he did. There was talk of running him for the state senate.

All in all, you might say the Stone family was as happy and contented as cats in a dairy. And so they were—except for Jabez Stone.

He'd been contented enough the first few years. It's a great thing when bad luck turns good. It drives most other things out of your head.

True, every now and then the little white scar on his finger would hurt a bit. And once a year, regular as a clock, the stranger with the handsome buggy would come driving by.

The sixth year the stranger stopped. After that, Jabez Stone's peace was over.

The stranger came up through the lower field. He wore handsome black boots which he tapped with a cane as he walked. Jabez Stone never liked the look of those boots, particularly the toes.

The stranger passed the time of day for a while. Then he said, "Well, Mr. Stone, you're a busy man! It's a very pretty property you've got here, Mr. Stone."

"Well, some might like it and others might not," said Jabez Stone. After all, he was a New Hampshireman.

"Oh, no need to make light of your efforts," said the stranger smoothly, showing his teeth in a smile. "After all, we know what's been done. And it's been done just according to the details of the contract. So when—ahem—the mortgage[3] falls due next year, you shouldn't have any regrets."

"Speaking of that mortgage, mister," Jabez began. He looked around for help to the earth and sky. "I'm beginning to have one or two doubts about it."

"Doubts?" said the stranger. His tone was not quite so pleasant.

"Why, yes," said Jabez Stone. "This being the U.S.A. and me always having been a religious man." He cleared his throat and got bolder.

"Yes, sir," he said, "I'm beginning to really doubt if that mortgage would hold up in court."

"There's courts and courts," said the stranger, clicking his teeth. "Still, we might as well look at the original document."

He hauled out a big black pocketbook full of papers. "Sherwin, Slater, Stevens, Stone," he muttered. " 'I, Jabez Stone, for a term of seven years—' Oh, it's quite in order, I think."

But Jabez Stone wasn't listening. He saw something else flutter out of the black pocketbook. It was something that looked like a moth, but it wasn't a moth.

As Jabez Stone stared at it, it seemed to speak to him in a small, high-pitched voice. The voice was terribly small and thin but terribly human.

---

[3]A mortgage is a deed that gives someone a claim to property in case a debt is not repaid.

"Neighbor Stone!" the voice squeaked. "Neighbor Stone! Help me! For God's sake, help me!"

But before Jabez Stone could move, the stranger whipped out a big handkerchief. He caught the creature in it like a butterfly and started tying up the ends of the handkerchief.

"Sorry for the interruption," he said. "As I was saying—"

Jabez Stone was shaking all over like a scared horse.

"That's Miser Stevens' voice!" he croaked. "And you've got him in your handkerchief!"

The stranger looked a little embarrassed.

"Yes, I really should have **transferred** him to the collecting box," he said with a smirk. "But there were some rather rare **specimens** in there. I didn't want them crowded. Well, well, these unpleasant little accidents will happen."

"I don't know what you mean by accidents," Jabez Stone said. "But that was Miser Stevens' voice! And he ain't dead! You can't tell me he is! He was just as lively and mean as a woodchuck on Tuesday!"

"In the midst of life—" said the stranger in a kind of **pious** way. "Listen!"

Then a bell began to ring in the valley. Jabez Stone listened with the sweat running down his face. He knew it rang for Miser Stevens and that he was dead.

"These old accounts," said the stranger with a sigh. "One really hates to close them. But business is business."

He still had the handkerchief in his hand. And Jabez Stone felt sick as he saw the cloth struggle and flutter.

"Are they all as small as that?" he asked in a rough, dry voice.

"Small?" said the stranger. "Oh, I see what you mean. Why, they vary." He sized up Jabez Stone with his eyes, and his teeth showed.

"Don't worry, Mr. Stone," he said. "You'll be with a very good group. I wouldn't trust you outside the collecting box.

"Now, a man like Dan'l Webster, of course—well, we'd have to build a special box for him. Even at that, I imagine the wing spread would astonish you.

"He'd certainly be a prize. I wish we could see our way clear to get him. But, in your case, as I was saying—"

"Put the handkerchief away!" said Jabez Stone. And he began to beg and to pray. But the best he could get was an extra three years with conditions.

Till you make a bargain like that, you've got no idea how fast the years can go by. By the last months of those years, Jabez Stone was known all over the state. There was talk of running him for governor. But it was dust and ashes in Jabez's mouth.

Every day when he got up, he thought, "There's one more night gone." And every night when he lay down, he thought of the black pocketbook and the soul of Miser Stevens. It made him sick at heart.

Finally he couldn't bear it any longer. In the last days of his last year, he hitched up his horse and drove off to find Dan'l Webster.

You see, Dan'l was born in New Hampshire near Cross Corners. And it was well known that he had a special soft spot for his old neighbors.

It was early morning when Jabez got to Marshfield. But Dan'l was up already. He was talking Latin to the farmhands and wrestling with the ram, Goliath. He was trying out a new racehorse and working up speeches against John C. Calhoun.[4]

But when he heard a New Hampshireman had come to see him, he dropped everything. That was Dan'l's way. He gave Jabez Stone a breakfast that five men couldn't eat. Then he told him the life story of every person in Cross

[4]John C. Calhoun (1782-1850) was a well-known statesman and opponent of Daniel Webster. Calhoun supported the South and states' rights.

Corners. Finally he asked how he could help Jabez Stone.

Jabez Stone said that it was a kind of mortgage case.

"Well, I haven't taken a mortgage case in years," Dan'l said. "I don't generally go to court now, except the Supreme Court. But if I can, I'll help you."

"Then I've got hope for the first time in ten years," said Jabez Stone. And he told him the details.

Dan'l walked up and down with his hands behind his back as he listened. Now and then he asked a question. Sometimes he stared at the floor as if he'd drill through it with his eyes.

When Jabez Stone had finished, Dan'l puffed out his cheeks and blew. Then he turned to Jabez Stone. A smile broke over his face like the sunrise over Monadnock.[5]

"You've sure given yourself the devil's own row to hoe, Neighbor Stone," he said. "But I'll take your case."

"You'll take it?" said Jabez Stone. He hardly dared believe it.

"Yes," said Dan'l Webster. "I've got about seventy-five other things to do. And there's the Missouri **Compromise**[6] to straighten out. But I'll take your case. For if two New Hampshiremen aren't a match for the devil, we might as well give the country back to the Indians."

Then he shook Jabez Stone by the hand. "Did you come down here in a hurry?" he asked.

"Well, I admit I made time," said Jabez Stone.

"You'll go back faster," said Dan'l Webster. He told his help to hitch up Constitution and Constellation to the buggy. They were matching gray horses. Each had one white foot in front. And they stepped like greased lightning.

On the trip back, Jabez Stone lost his hat. It blew off when they overtook a wind. But he didn't take much notice of that.

Well, I won't describe how excited and pleased the Stone family was to have the great Dan'l Webster for a guest. But

[5]Monadnock is a famous mountain in New Hampshire.

[6]The Missouri Compromise was a plan passed by Congress (1820-21) to keep a balance between slave states and free states.

after supper, Jabez sent the family to bed. He had important business with Mr. Webster.

Mrs. Stone wanted them to sit in the front sitting room. But Dan'l Webster knew front sitting rooms and said he preferred the kitchen.

So there they sat, waiting for the stranger. They had a jug on the table between them. There was a bright fire in the fireplace. The stranger was to show up on the stroke of midnight, according to the contract.

Well, most men wouldn't have asked for better company than Dan'l Webster and a jug. But Jabez Stone grew sadder and sadder with every tick of the clock. His eyes wandered around. Though he took sips from the jug, you could see he wasn't even tasting it.

Finally, at 11:30, he reached over and grabbed Dan'l Webster's arm.

"Mr. Webster, Mr. Webster!" he said. His voice was shaking with fear and reckless courage. "For God's sake, Mr. Webster, hitch up your horses. Get away from this place while you can!"

"You've brought me a long way, neighbor, to tell me you don't like my company," said Dan'l Webster calmly. He took a drink from the jug.

"I'm a miserable **wretch**," groaned Jabez Stone. "I've brought you a terribly long way. Now I see I was a fool.

"Let him take me if he wants. I'm not longing for that, I must say, but I can stand it. But you're the support of the Union. And New Hampshire's pride! He mustn't get you, Mr. Webster! He mustn't get you!"

Dan'l Webster looked at the upset man, who was gray and shaking in the firelight. Dan'l laid a hand on his shoulder.

"I thank you, Neighbor Stone," he said gently. "That's a kind thought. But there's a jug on the table and a case at hand. And I never left a jug or a case half finished in my life.''

Just at that moment there was a sharp knock on the door.

''Ah,'' said Dan'l Webster very coolly. ''I thought your clock was a little slow, Neighbor Stone.'' He stepped to the door and opened it. ''Come in,'' he said.

The stranger came in. He looked very tall and dark in the firelight. He was carrying a box under his arm. It was black and varnished, with little air holes in the lid. Jabez Stone gave a low cry and shrank into a corner of the room.

''Mr. Webster, I would guess,'' said the stranger very politely. But his eyes glowed like a fox's deep in the woods.

''Lawyer for Jabez Stone,'' said Dan'l Webster. His eyes were glowing, too. ''Might I ask your name?''

''I've gone by many,'' said the stranger carelessly. ''Perhaps Scratch will do for the evening. I'm often called that around here.''

Then he sat down at the table and poured himself a drink. The liquor was cold in the jug. But it steamed in the glass.

''And now,'' said the stranger, smiling and showing his teeth, ''I ask you as a law-**abiding** citizen to help me take possession of my property.''

Well, with that the argument began. It went hot and heavy. At first Jabez Stone had a flicker of hope. But when he saw Dan'l Webster losing point after point, he just sat huddled in his corner. And he kept his eyes on the black varnished box.

There wasn't any doubt about the deed or the signature. That was the worst of it. Dan'l Webster twisted and turned. He thumped his fist on the table. But he couldn't get away from that.

He offered a compromise. The stranger wouldn't hear of it. He pointed out that the property had increased in value. State senators should be worth more than farmers. But the stranger stuck to the letter of the law.

Dan'l Webster was a great lawyer. But we all know who is the King of Lawyers, as the Bible tells us. For the first time, it looked like Dan'l Webster had met his match.

Finally the stranger yawned a little. "Your spirited efforts on the part of your client show you to be a fine man, Mr. Webster," he said. "But if you have no more arguments to present, I'm in rather a hurry—" Jabez Stone shook.

Dan'l Webster's forehead looked dark as a thundercloud.

"In a hurry or not, you shall not have this man!" he thundered. "Mr. Stone is an American citizen. And no American citizen may be forced to serve a foreign prince. We fought England for that in '12.[7] And we'll fight all hell for it again!"

"Foreign?" said the stranger. "And who calls me a foreigner?"

"Well, I never yet heard of the dev—of you saying you were an American citizen," said Dan'l Webster with surprise.

"And who has a better right?" said the stranger. He smiled one of his terrible smiles. "When the first wrong was done to the first Indian, I was there. When the first slave ship set off for the African Congo, I stood on her deck.

"Am I not in your books and stories and beliefs since the first towns were settled? Am I not spoken of still in every church in New England?

"True, the North calls me a Southerner, and the South says I'm a Northerner. But I am neither. I am merely an honest American like you, Mr. Webster.

"I have an excellent background, too. I don't like to boast about it. But to tell the truth, Mr. Webster, my name is older in this country than yours!"

"Aha!" said Dan'l Webster. The veins were now standing out on his forehead. "Then I stand on the Constitution! I demand a trial for my client!"

---

[7]The War of 1812 started in part because the English forced some American sailors into serving on British ships.

"The case is hardly one for an ordinary court," said the stranger. His eyes flickered. "And in view of how late it is—"

"Let it be any court you choose. Just let it be an American judge and an American jury!" said Dan'l Webster proudly. "Let them be living or dead. I'll abide by their decision."

"You have said it," said the stranger. He pointed his finger at the door.

With that, there was a sudden rush of wind and a noise of footsteps outside. They came, clear and **distinct**, through the night. And yet they were not like the footsteps of living men.

"In God's name, who is coming here so late at night?" cried Jabez Stone, sick with fear.

"The jury Mr. Webster demands," said the stranger. He sipped at his boiling glass. "You must pardon the rough way that one or two of them look. They will have come a long way."

And with that the fire burned blue, and the door blew open. Twelve dead men entered, one by one.

If Jabez Stone had been sick with terror before, he was blind with terror now. For there was Walter Butler, the British supporter. He had spread fire and horror through the Mohawk Valley during the Revolution.

And there was Simon Girty, the **renegade**. He saw white men burned at the stake. And he whooped with the Indians to see them burn. His eyes were green like a mountain lion's. The stains on his hunting shirt were not from the blood of deer.

The wild, proud King Philip was there. He had the huge gash in his head that had caused his death.

Cruel Governor Dale was there, too. He had tortured and killed men.

There was Morton of Merry Mount. He had troubled the

Plymouth Colony and had hated the godly. He had a red, fleshy, handsome face.

There was Teach, the bloody pirate. His black beard lay curling on his chest.

And in came the Reverend John Smeet, the strangler. He walked with just the same dainty step as he had to the gallows. The red mark the rope had left was still around his neck. But he carried a perfumed handkerchief in one hand.

One and all, they came into the room with the fires of hell still upon them. The stranger told the names and deeds of each of the twelve as they entered.

Yet the stranger had told the truth. All twelve had played a part in American history.

"Are you satisfied with the jury, Mr. Webster?" said the stranger **mockingly** when they had taken their places.

There was sweat on Dan'l Webster's forehead. But his voice was clear. "Quite satisfied," he said. "Though I see General Arnold is missing from the group."

"Benedict Arnold has other business," said the stranger with a frown. "Ah, you asked for a judge, I believe."

He pointed his finger once more. A tall man in dark Puritan clothes entered. His eyes had the burning gaze of a **fanatic**. He marched into the room and took his place as judge.

"Judge Hathorne has much experience as a judge," said the stranger. "He ruled at some witch trials once held in Salem. Other people were sorry for their part in the business later. But he was not."

"Sorry for such famous wonders and actions?" said the stern old judge. "No, hang them. Hang them all!" And he muttered to himself in a way that made Jabez Stone's soul turn to ice.

Then the trial began. As you might expect, it didn't look good at all for Jabez Stone. And Jabez didn't make a very good witness for himself. He took one look at Simon Girty and screamed. They had to put him back in the corner, half fainting.

That didn't halt the trial though. The trial went on, as trials do. Dan'l Webster had faced some hard juries and hanging judges in his time. But this was the hardest he'd ever faced. And he knew it. They sat there with a kind of glitter in their eyes.

The stranger's smooth voice went on and on. Every time he raised an objection, the judge would agree. But whenever Dan'l Webster would object, the judge would disagree. Well, you couldn't expect fair play from a fellow like this Mr. Scratch.

It was Dan'l's turn in the end. He began to heat up like an iron in the flames. He decided that when he spoke, he was going to whip the stranger with every trick he knew. And he was going to let the judge and jury have it, too.

He didn't care if he was ruled in contempt of court.[8] He didn't care what happened to him. He didn't care anymore what happened to Jabez Stone. He just got madder and madder, thinking of what he'd say.

And yet it was strange. The more he thought about it, the less he was able to plan his speech.

Finally it was time for him to get up and speak. He stood up, ready to bust out with lightning and criticisms.

But before he started, he looked over at the judge and jury. This was his custom. And he noticed that the glitter in their eyes was twice as strong as before.

They were all leaning forward. They looked like hounds, just before they get the fox. The blue mist of evil in the room grew thicker as he watched them.

Then Dan'l Webster saw what he'd been about to do. He wiped his forehead the way a man might who had just escaped falling into a pit in the dark.

For it was him they'd come for, not only Jabez Stone.

---

[8]Contempt of court is the act of disobeying or showing a lack of respect for court rules.

He saw it in the glitter of their eyes. He saw it in the way the stranger hid his mouth with one hand.

And if he fought them with their own weapons, he'd fall into their power. He knew that, though he couldn't have told you how. It was his own anger and horror that burned in their eyes. He'd have to wipe that out or the case was lost.

He stood there for a minute. His black eyes burned like coal. Then he began to speak.

He started off in a low voice. But you could hear every word. They say he could call on the harps of heaven when he chose. To do this was just as simple and easy as a man could talk. He didn't **condemn** or scold. He talked about the things that make a country a country and a man a man.

He began with the simple things that everybody's known and felt. The freshness of a fine morning when you're young. And the taste of food when you're hungry. He said that every day seemed a new day when you're a child.

He took these things up and turned them in his hands. They were good things for anyone.

But without freedom, they grew sick. And when he talked about slaves and what sadness slavery brought, his voice rang like a big bell. He talked of the early days of America and the people who had made those days.

It wasn't a flag-waving speech, but he made you see it. He admitted all the wrong that had ever been done. But he showed how something new had come out of wrong and right, out of pain and hunger. And everybody had played a part in it, even the traitors.

Then he turned to Jabez Stone. He showed him as he was—an ordinary man who had had hard luck and wanted to change it. And because of that wish, he was going to be punished for all **eternity**.

And yet there was good in Jabez Stone. Dan'l showed that good. Jabez was hard and mean, in some ways. But he was a man. There was sadness in being human, but it was a proud thing, too.

Dan'l showed what that pride was till you couldn't help feeling it. Yes, even in hell, if a man was a real man, you'd know it.

And he wasn't pleading for any one person anymore. He was telling the story, the failures, and the endless journey of mankind. Human beings got tricked and trapped and fooled. But it was a great journey. And no demon ever born could know how it felt. It took a human being to do that.

The fire began to die in the fireplace. The wind before morning began to blow. The light was getting gray in the room when Dan'l finished. At the end, he talked about New Hampshire. He talked about the one spot of land that each person loves and clings to.

Dan'l painted a picture of that. Then he spoke of things long forgotten to each one of the jury. His voice could search the heart. That was his gift and his strength.

To one, his voice was like a forest and its secrets. To another, it was like the sea and its storms. One heard the cry of his lost nation. Another saw some little harmless scene he hadn't remembered for years. But each saw something.

When Dan'l Webster finished, he didn't know if he'd saved Jabez Stone. But he knew he'd done a miracle. For the glitter was gone from the eyes of the judge and jury. For the moment, they were men again. And they knew it.

"I rest my case," said Dan'l Webster. He stood there like a mountain. His ears were still ringing with his speech. He didn't hear anything else till he heard Judge Hathorne say, "The jury will go into the other room to come to a **verdict**."

Walter Butler stood up. His face had a dark, glowing pride on it.

"The jury has reached its verdict," he said. He looked the stranger directly in the eye. "We rule in favor of Jabez Stone."

With that, the smile left the stranger's face. But Walter Butler did not flinch.

"It may not be in line with the evidence," Butler said. "But even the damned may salute the **eloquence** of Mr. Webster."

With that, a rooster's long crow split the gray morning sky. And judge and jury were gone from the room like a puff of smoke. It was as if they had never been there.

With a twisted smile, the stranger turned to Dan'l Webster.

"Major Butler was always a bold man," he said. "I did not know how bold. Well, from one gentleman to another, congratulations."

"I'll have that paper first, if you please," said Dan'l Webster. He took it and tore it into four pieces. It was strangely warm to the touch. "And now," he said, "I'll have you!"

His hand came down like a bear trap on the stranger's arm. He knew that once you beat someone like Mr. Scratch in a fair fight, his power over you was gone. He could see that Mr. Scratch knew it, too.

The stranger twisted and wriggled. But he couldn't get out of that grip.

"Come, come, Mr. Webster," he said, smiling weakly. "This sort of thing is ridic—ouch!—is ridiculous. If you're worried about the costs of the case, naturally I'd be glad to pay—"

"And so you shall!" said Dan'l Webster. He shook the stranger until his teeth rattled.

"You're going to sit right down at that table and write out a document. You'll promise never to bother Jabez Stone or his **heirs** or any other citizen of New Hampshire till the end of time!

"Any hell we want to raise in this state, we can raise ourselves. We don't need help from strangers."

"Ouch!" said the stranger. "Ouch! Well they never were very big sinners here. But—ouch!—I agree!"

So he sat down and wrote the document. But Dan'l Webster kept hold of the stranger's coat collar all the time.

Afterwards, Dan'l checked to see that the document was in proper and legal form. Then the stranger said in a humble way, "And now may I go?"

"Go?" said Dan'l, giving him another shake. "I'm still trying to figure out what I'll do with you. You've settled the costs of the case. But you haven't settled with me.

"I think I'll take you back to Marshfield," he said in a thoughtful way. "I've got a ram there named Goliath. He can butt through an iron door. I'd like to turn you loose in his field and see what he'd do."

Well, the stranger began to beg and plead when he heard that. And he begged and he pled so humbly that kindhearted Dan'l finally agreed to let him go.

The stranger seemed very grateful and said he'd tell Dan'l's fortune before leaving. So Dan'l agreed to that. He didn't usually believe in fortunetellers. But, naturally, the stranger was a little different.

Well, he **pried** and peered at the lines in Dan'l's hands. And he told him some quite remarkable things. But they were all in the past.

"Yes, all that's true. It happened," said Dan'l. "But what's to come in the future?"

The stranger grinned kind of happily and shook his head.

"The future's not as you think," he said. "It's dark. You have a great **ambition**, Mr. Webster."

"I have," said Dan'l firmly. Everybody knew he wanted to be president.

"It seems almost within your grasp," said the stranger. "But it won't be yours. Men who are not as great as you are will be made president. You will be passed over."

"And, if I am, I'll still be Daniel Webster," said Dan'l. "Go on."

"You have two strong sons," said the stranger, shaking his head. "You hope that your family line will go on for a long time. But each son will die in war. Neither will reach greatness."

"Live or die, they are still my sons," said Dan'l Webster. "Go on."

"You have made great speeches," said the stranger. "You will make more."

"Ah," said Dan'l Webster.

"But the last great speech you make will turn many of your supporters against you," said the stranger. "They will call you Ichabod.[9]

"They will call you other names. Even in New England, some will say you are a turncoat and have sold your country. Their voices will be loud against you till you die."

"If it is an honest speech, it doesn't matter what people say," said Dan'l Webster. Then he looked at the stranger. Their glances locked.

"One question," Dan'l said. "I have fought for the Union all my life. Will I see that fight won against those who would tear it apart?"

"Not while you live," said the stranger **grimly**. "But it will be won. And after you are dead, thousands will fight for your cause because of the words you spoke."

Dan'l Webster gave a great roar of laughter. "Why, then, you long-barreled, slab-sided, lantern-jawed, fortunetelling cheater, be off with you!" he said. "Get back to your own place before I hit you! For, I swear by the thirteen original colonies, I'd go to hell itself to save the Union!"

And with that, he drew back his foot for a kick that would have stunned a horse. Only the tip of his shoe caught the stranger. But he went flying out the door with his collecting box under his arm.

---

[9]Ichabod means "the glory is gone from Israel." Ichabod is a Biblical character. He was born after a battle which Israel lost.

"Well, now," said Dan'l Webster, seeing that Jabez Stone was recovering from his faint. "Let's see what's left in the jug. It's dry work talking all night. I hope there's pie for breakfast, Neighbor Stone."

They say that whenever the devil comes near Marshfield, he steers clear of it even now. And he hasn't been seen in New Hampshire from that day to this. I'm not talking about Massachusetts or Vermont.

"The Devil and Daniel Webster" was first published in 1937.

INSIGHTS INTO
STEPHEN VINCENT BENET

(1893-1943)

Benet's "The Devil and Daniel Webster" is not only a famous short story. The tale has been so popular that it was turned into a stage and TV play, an opera, and a motion picture.

Benet was very fond of reading. From his childhood until his death, he usually began a book or finished one each day.

Benet won his first cash award for a poem when he was 13. He published his first volume of poetry when he was 17. In all, he published over seventeen volumes of poetry and prose.

Benet knew his poor eyesight would keep him out of the army in World War I. So he memorized the eye chart.

But when a sergeant spotted Benet trying to peel potatoes, the game was up. Benet was discharged after only three days in the service. He went on to serve in the State Department as a code clerk. He worked in the same office as author James Thurber.

Benet was a tireless patriot. Before and during World War II, he was often ill. But Benet never gave up trying to boost the spirits of Americans with his writing.

Benet also had a policy of never taking money for his war work. Once when he said he had "no money, and owe more than in a long time," he received a check for $500 from *Life* magazine. Since the check was for a patriotic script, Benet sent the money to the USO.

Benet won the Pulitzer Prize for his Civil War poem, *John Brown's Body*. He won another Pulitzer, after his death, for his poem *Western Star*.

Other works by Benet:
   "By the Waters of Babylon," short story
   "The Curfew Tolls," short story
   "Johnny Pye and the Foolkiller," short story
   A Book of Americans, poetry collection
    (co-written by Rosemary Benet)

THE LADY
OR THE TIGER?

FRANK STOCKTON

VOCABULARY PREVIEW

Below is a list of words that appear in the story. Read the list and get to know the words before you start the story.

advanced—moved forward
agony—great suffering
anguished—feeling pain or sorrow
anxiety—concern and uneasiness
assured—certain; confident
barbaric—not civilized; like a savage
crouched—hunched and bent low
cultured—educated to understand art, music, etc.
destiny—one's fate or end
devious—twisting and roundabout
devoured—ate with hunger and greed
emerge—come out
idealism—believing in and following what one thinks is perfect or best
influenced—persuaded to act or think in a certain way
intense—fierce or strong
interfere—to butt in
mourners—people, especially those at a funeral, who grieve over a dead person
slaughter—a bloody killing without mercy
surveyed—looked over; examined
waver—to show uncertainty; hesitate

THE LADY OR THE TIGER?

FRANK STOCKTON

In the king's arena, the accused sets his own fate by opening one of two doors. What awaits him there is the deepest of secrets.
But what happens when one fiery woman learns that secret? Which will she unleash on the accused: the lady or the tiger?

In the very old days, there lived a king who was semi-**barbaric**. His ideas had been somewhat polished and sharpened by civilized Latin[1] neighbors. But these ideas were still large, high sounding, and untamed.

This suited the king's barbaric half. He was a man of rich, lively imagination. And because his power was so great, he could turn his fantasies into facts when he wanted.

He had a habit of talking things over with himself. And when he and himself agreed on anything, the thing was done.

---

[1]Latin refers to the nations and people who speak languages developed from Latin. France, Spain, Portugal, and Italy are some of the Latin countries.

When everyone in his household and kingdom smoothly did their duties, the king was good-natured and cheerful. But whenever there was a little hitch, he was even more polite and cheerful. You see, nothing pleased him more than making the crooked straight and the rocky places smooth.

One of the borrowed ideas that made him less barbaric was the public arena. There he held shows of courage by man and beast. These shows improved and **cultured** the minds of his subjects.

But even here his lively and barbaric imagination could be seen. The arena of the king was not built to give the people a chance to hear the brave cries of dying gladiators.[2] Nor was it built to let them view the outcome of a conflict between religious opinions and hungry jaws. Instead, the arena was built for purposes far more likely to widen and develop the minds of the people.

In this huge amphitheatre[3] were circling rows of seats, mysterious cellars, and unseen passages. The arena was a place where a fitting kind of justice was given out. There crime was punished or goodness rewarded. The decision depended on the fair and unbreakable laws of chance.

Sometimes a subject was accused of a crime important enough to interest the king. Then the public was told when the fate of the accused would be decided in the king's arena.

The king's arena well deserved its name. It is true that its form and plan were borrowed from a far-off land. But the purpose of the arena sprang from the king's brain alone. Since he was every inch a king, he was loyal to whatever pleased his imagination. He added his own rich, barbaric **idealism** to every foreign idea and action.

On trial days, all the people gathered in the stands. The king, surrounded by his court,[4] sat high up on his throne

---

[2]Gladiators are men who were trained to fight in arenas before the public.

[3]An amphitheatre is a large, round building with seats circling an arena in the center.

[4]A court is the family, close followers, and advisers of a monarch.

on one side of the arena. When he gave a signal, a door beneath him opened. The accused person stepped out into the amphitheatre.

Directly across from the king were two doors. Those doors were exactly alike and stood side by side. It was the prisoner's duty and right to walk directly to the doors and open one of them. He could open either door he pleased. He was not guided or **influenced** except by those fair and unbreakable laws of chance.

If he opened the one door, out came a hungry tiger—the fiercest and most cruel available. It immediately sprang on him. He would be torn to pieces as a punishment for his guilt.

The moment the criminal's case was decided this way, sad iron bells were clanged. From the edges of the arena, hired **mourners** cried loudly. The huge audience slowly made their way home with bowed heads and sad hearts. They mourned that one so young and handsome, or so old and respected, had earned such a terrible fate.

But if the accused subject opened the other door, out stepped a lady. This lady was a woman selected by his Majesty. She was chosen as being the most suitable in age and class to the prisoner. The prisoner was immediately married to this lady as a reward for his innocence.

It did not matter if the man already had a wife and family. It did not matter if he loved someone he had chosen himself. The king let no arrangements like these **interfere** with his great plan of punishment and reward.

The marriage took place immediately and in the arena. Another door opened beneath the king, and a priest entered. He was followed by a band of singers and dancing maidens. The maidens blew joyful tunes on golden horns and danced a wedding step. They **advanced** to where the pair stood side by side. And there the wedding was performed quickly and cheerily.

Then the joyful brass bells rang merrily. The people would shout gladly, too. As children scattered flowers in his path, the innocent man led his bride to his home.

This was the king's semi-barbaric way of handing out justice. Its perfect fairness is obvious. The criminal could not know out of which door the lady would come. He opened either door he pleased. He did not have the slightest idea whether in the next instant he was to be **devoured** or married.

Sometimes the tiger came out of one door, sometimes the other. The decisions of this lawcourt were not only fair— they also settled things once and for all. The accused person was instantly punished if he found himself guilty. If innocent, he was rewarded on the spot, whether he liked it or not. There was no escape from the judgments of the king's arena.

This practice was a very popular one. The people who gathered for the trials never knew if they would see a bloody **slaughter** or a cheerful wedding.

This element of uncertainty is what made the occasion so interesting. In this way the common people were entertained and pleased. And the thinkers in the kingdom could not say this plan was unfair. Didn't the accused person have the whole matter in his own hands?

This semi-barbaric king had a daughter. She was as blooming as his most flowery ideas. And her soul was as fiery and masterful as her father's. Naturally, she was the apple of his eye. He loved her above all humanity.

In the king's court there was a young man of good family and low rank. These were common traits for the traditional heroes of romance who loved royal maidens.

This royal maiden was well satisfied with her lover. After all, he was the handsomest and bravest in all the kingdom. She loved him with a passion made extremely warm and strong because it was partly barbaric.

This love affair moved on happily for many months. Then, one day, the king happened to discover it. He did not hesitate or **waver** in doing his duty in the case. The youth was immediately thrown into prison. And a day was set for his trial in the king's arena.

This, of course, was quite an important occasion. Both his Majesty and all the people were greatly interested in the development of this trial. Never before had such a case occurred. Never before had a subject dared to love the daughter of the king. Such things became commonplace in later years. But then they were quite new and startling.

The tiger cages of the kingdom were searched for the most savage and cruel beasts. From these, the fiercest monster would be selected for the arena.

Skillful judges also carefully **surveyed** the young and beautiful maidens in the land. This was done so the young man might have a fitting bride if fate did not choose a different **destiny** for him.

Of course, everybody knew that the accused had really done the deed he was charged with. He had loved the princess. Neither he, she, nor anyone else thought of denying the fact. But the king would not let this interfere with the way his lawcourt worked.

No matter how things turned out, the youth would be taken care of. The king would take an artistic pleasure in watching the events which would determine the young man's guilt.

The day that had been chosen arrived. From far and near the people gathered and overflowed the great stands of the arena. Crowds who could not get inside pressed against the outside walls. The king and his court were in their places. They sat opposite the twin doors—those doors of fate, so fearful in their similarity!

All was ready. The signal was given. A door beneath the

royal group opened. Then the lover of the princess walked into the arena, tall and handsome.

The crowd greeted him with a low hum of admiration and **anxiety**. Half of the audience had not known that so grand a youth lived among them. No wonder the princess loved him! What a terrible thing for him to be there!

The youth advanced into the arena. He turned, as was the custom, to bow to the king. But he did not think of the king at all. His eyes were fixed upon the princess, who sat to the right of her father.

If it hadn't been for the barbaric half of her nature, the lady would probably not have been there. But her **intense** and fiery spirit would not let her miss an occasion in which she was so interested. Ever since she heard that her lover must be tried in the arena, she had thought of nothing else. Night and day, she thought about only this great event.

She had more power, influence, and determination than anyone who had ever been interested in such a case. As a result, she had done what no other person had done. She had learned the secret of the doors. She knew behind which door the tiger's cage stood open and behind which the lady waited.

These thick doors were heavily curtained with skins on the inside. It was impossible for any noise from within to reach the person who would raise the latch. But gold and the power of a woman's will had brought the secret to the princess.

The princess not only knew in which room the blushing and glowing lady stood, ready to **emerge**. She also knew who that lady was. One of the fairest and loveliest maidens of the court had been chosen as the accused youth's reward. But first he must be proved innocent of the crime of desiring someone so far above him.

The princess hated the maiden. She had often seen, or imagined she had seen, this fair creature admiring the

princess' lover. Sometimes she thought her lover noticed and even returned these admiring looks.

Now and then the princess had seen them talking together. It was only for a moment or two. Yet, much can be said in a brief time. They might have talked of unimportant topics. But how could she know that?

The girl was lovely, but she had dared to gaze at the princess' loved one. The princess' blood, which had passed down to her from a long line of barbaric ancestors, was fierce. She intensely hated the woman who blushed and trembled behind that silent door.

Now the princess' lover turned and looked at her. His eye met hers. She sat there paler and whiter than anyone in the huge ocean of anxious faces around her. Because their souls were still united as one, he saw at once that she knew the secret. She knew behind which door **crouched** the tiger and behind which stood the lady.

He had expected her to know it. He understood her nature. His soul was **assured** she would never rest until she learned this thing hidden to all others, even to the king. This was the youth's only certain hope—that the princess would discover the mystery. And the moment he looked at her, he saw she had succeeded.

And then his quick and anxious glance asked the question, "Which?" His silent question was as plain to her as if he had shouted it. There was not an instant to be lost. The question was asked in a flash. It must be answered in another.

Her right arm lay on the cushioned railing in front of her. She raised her hand and made a slight, quick movement toward the right. No one but her lover saw her. Every eye but his was fixed on the man in the arena.

He turned and walked firmly and rapidly across the empty space. Every heart stopped beating. Every breath was held. Every eye was fixed on that man. Without the slightest pause, he went to the door on the right and opened it.

Now the point of the story is this: Did the tiger come out of that door or did the lady?

The more we think about this question, the harder it is to answer. It involves a study of the human heart. This leads us through **devious** mazes of passion. Those mazes are difficult to escape.

Think of it, fair reader, not as if the decision depended on you. But look at it from that hot-blooded, semi-barbaric princess' point of view. Think of her soul heated to a white-hot flame by the fires of hopelessness and jealousy. She had lost him, but who should have him?

Awake or asleep, how often had she thought of her lover opening the tiger's door. She had thought of how the cruel fangs waited! Then she would shake with wild horror and cover her face.

But how much oftener had she seen him at the other door in her troubling dreams! How she had ground her teeth and torn her hair when she saw his delight as he opened the door of the lady! How her soul had burned with **agony** when she had seen him rush to meet that woman. And how that woman's cheeks would flush and her eyes sparkle with victory!

Then the princess had seen him lead the lady forth. His whole body had been lit with the joy of recovered life. She had heard the glad shouts from the crowd and the wild ringing of the happy bells.

She had seen the priest, with his joyous followers, go to the couple. Then they became man and wife before her very eyes.

And she had seen them walk away together upon their path of flowers. Behind them the merry crowd followed with great shouting. And in all this, her one hopeless shriek was lost and drowned!

Would it not be better for him to die at once? Then he would go to wait for her in the blessed lands of the semi-barbaric hereafter.

And yet, that awful tiger! Those shrieks, that blood!

Her decision had been given in an instant. But it had been made after days and nights of **anguished** thought. She had known she would be asked. She had decided what she would answer. And so, without the slightest pause, she had moved her hand to the right.

The question of her decision is not one to be considered lightly. And it is not for me to set myself up as the one person able to answer it. So I leave it with all of you: Which came out of the opened door—the lady or the tiger?

"The Lady or the Tiger?" was first published in 1882.

INSIGHTS INTO FRANK STOCKTON

(1834-1902)

Before he was a full-time writer, Stockton made his living as a wood engraver. Later he engraved pictures for some of his own stories.

When "The Lady or the Tiger?" was published, Stockton was paid only $50 for writing it. But the story became very popular. The ending was debated around the country. Thousands wrote to Stockton. They begged him for a final answer to the story. But Stockton refused to give one. Instead he said, "If you decide which it was—the lady or the tiger—you find out what kind of person you are yourself."

Stockton had given the ending of "The Lady or the Tiger?" as much thought as his puzzled readers. Usually Stockton did not revise the first draft of a story. But in the case of "The Lady or the Tiger?", he rewrote the ending five times.

Though "The Lady or the Tiger?" made Stockton famous, it created problems for him. For a time, editor after editor refused other stories he sent them. They complained that none could match the dramatic "Lady or Tiger."

Stockton became assistant editor of *St. Nicholas Magazine,* a famous magazine for children. He worked long, hard hours at the magazine. But he still kept his sense of humor. Once he noticed that his boss had left her boots at the office. He wrapped them up and had them sent to her home. In

continued

the package he sent a rejection slip. It read, "Many articles must be returned for reasons which have no connection with literary merit."

Other works by Stockton:

"The Discourager of Hesitancy," short story
   (a sequel to "The Lady or the Tiger?")
"The Griffin and the Minor Canon," short story
"The Queen's Museum," short story
"The Transferred Ghost," short story
The Casting Away of Mrs. Lecks and Mrs. Aleshine, novel

DR. HEIDEGGER'S EXPERIMENT

NATHANIEL HAWTHORNE

VOCABULARY PREVIEW

Below is a list of words that appear in the story. Read the list and get to know the words before you start the story.

clustered—gathered in a small, close group; bunched
corpses—dead bodies
deception—trickery
delirium—wild excitement or enthusiasm; frenzy
disputed—questioned or challenged
elaborate—fancy and complex
fragile—easily broken; frail or brittle
impulse—urge or sudden desire
infamous—having a bad reputation
intoxicating—exciting to the point of making one lose self-control
mischievous—teasing; full of mischief
obscurest—darkest or most unclear
patriotism—loyalty to and support of one's country
perils—dangers; risks
prime—the best or most perfect part of life
skeptics—doubters or unbelievers
threatening—alarming and promising hurt; full of threats
venerable—old and respected
virtues—good qualities; merits
withered—dried up and shrunken

DR. HEIDEGGER'S EXPERIMENT

Nathaniel Hawthorne

Hawthorne once said, "Nobody will use other people's experience or any of their own till it is too late to use it." Dr. Heidegger puts this saying to the test. With one magical drink, his four old friends can return to youth. But will they take the lessons of old age with them?

That very unusual man, old Dr. Heidegger, once invited four **venerable** friends to meet him in his study. There were three white-bearded gentlemen—Mr. Medbourne, Colonel Killigrew, and Mr. Gascoigne. A **withered** old lady, whose name was Widow Wycherly, came also.

They were all sad old creatures who had been unlucky in life. Their worst luck was that they had not died long ago.

When he was young, Mr. Medbourne had been a well-to-do merchant. But he had lost everything he had by a wild investment. Now he was little better than a beggar.

Colonel Killigrew had wasted his best years—and his health and money—following after sinful pleasures. This had produced many types of pain, such as the gout,[1] and various other torments in his soul and body.

Mr. Gascoigne was a ruined politician, a man of evil fame. At least he had been known as this until time had passed by and people forgot him. Now he was unknown instead of **infamous**.

As for the Widow Wycherly, it is said that she had been a great beauty in her day. But for a long time, she had lived totally alone. Some shameful gossip made the wealthy people of the town look down upon her.

It is worth mentioning that each of these three old gentlemen—Mr. Medbourne, Colonel Killigrew, and Mr. Gascoigne—were early lovers of the Widow Wycherly. They had once been on the point of cutting each other's throats for her sake.

And before going on, I will merely hint that Dr. Heidegger and all of his four guests were sometimes thought to be a little crazy. This is commonly the case with old people when they worry about present troubles or sad memories.

"My dear old friends," said Dr. Heidegger, motioning them to be seated. "I want your help in one of those little experiments that I amuse myself with here in my study."

If all stories were true, Dr. Heidegger's study must have been a very strange place. It was a dim, old-fashioned room. It was hung with cobwebs and sprinkled with old dust.

Around the walls stood several oak bookcases. The lower shelves were filled with rows of huge volumes and German books. The upper shelves held little books covered in parchment.[2]

---

[1]Gout is a disease which causes the swelling of the joints, especially in the fingers, knees, and toes.

[2]Parchment is a paperlike material made from the skin of a sheep, goat, etc.

Over the center bookcase was a bronze statue of Hippocrates.[3] Some knowledgeable people said Dr. Heidegger asked the statue's advice about all his difficult medical cases.

In the **obscurest** corner of the room stood a tall and narrow oak closet. Its door was open slightly, and a skeleton appeared to be hanging inside.

Between two of the bookcases hung a mirror. Its high and dusty glass was placed within a faded gold frame. Many wonderful stories were told about this mirror. It was said that the spirits of all the doctor's dead patients lived inside. They would stare him in the face whenever he looked there.

The opposite side of the room was decorated with the full-length portrait of a young lady. She was wearing a gorgeous but faded dress of silk, satin, and lace. Her face was as faded as her dress.

Over half a century ago, Dr. Heidegger had been on the point of marrying this young lady. But she had felt a little ill and had swallowed one of her lover's medicines. She died on the evening before her wedding.

I still have not mentioned the strangest thing in the study. It was a heavy volume covered in black leather and with huge silver clasps. There were no letters on the back, and nobody could tell the title of the book. But it was well known to be a book of magic.

Once a maid had lifted the book just to brush away the dust. Then the skeleton had rattled in its closet. The young lady in the picture had stepped out onto the floor with one foot, also. And several hideous faces had peeped out of the mirror. At the same time, the bronze head of Hippocrates had frowned and said, "Stop!"

That was Dr. Heidegger's study. On the summer afternoon of our story, a small, round table stood in the center of the room. On its black top stood a beautiful and **elaborate** cut-glass vase. The sunshine came through the window between the two heavy, faded, silk curtains. It fell on this vase

---

[3]Hippocrates (460-377 B.C.) was a Greek doctor who is known as the father of medicine.

so that a lovely reflection lit the pale faces of the five old people who sat around. Four champagne glasses were also on the table.

"My dear old friends," said Dr. Heidegger again, "can I count on your aid in carrying out a very odd experiment?"

Now Dr. Heidegger was a very strange old gentleman. His strangeness had become the center of a thousand fantastic stories. I am ashamed to admit that some of these fables might be traced back to my own truthful self. Some parts of this tale might shake the reader's faith in me. If so, I will have to accept being called a teller of tall tales.

When the doctor's guests heard him suggest the experiment, they thought he planned nothing more amazing than the murder of a mouse in an air pump. Or perhaps they thought he was going to examine a cobweb under the microscope. He was always bothering his friends with some nonsense like that.

But without waiting for a reply, Dr. Heidegger limped across the room. He returned with that heavy book in black leather, which was said to be a book of magic.

Undoing the silver clasps, he opened the volume. From between its pages, he took a rose, or what was once a rose. Now the green leaves and red petals had turned brown. The ancient flower seemed ready to crumble to dust in the doctor's hands.

"This rose," said Dr. Heidegger with a sigh, "this same withered and crumbling flower, blossomed fifty-five years ago. It was given to me by Sylvia Ward. Her portrait hangs over there. I was going to wear it in my buttonhole at our wedding.

"For fifty-five years it has been treasured between the pages of this old volume. Now, would you think it possible that this rose—which is half a century old—could ever bloom again?"

"Nonsense!" said the Widow Wycherly with an annoyed toss of her head. "You might as well ask if an old woman's wrinkled face could ever bloom again."

"See!" answered Dr. Heidegger.

He uncovered the vase and threw the faded rose into the water inside. At first the flower lay lightly on top of the liquid. It did not seem to drink up any of the moisture.

Soon, however, a remarkable change began to be seen. The crushed and dried petals stirred and became a deeper color of red. It seemed as if the flower were awakening from a deathlike sleep. The slender stem and leaves became green.

There was the rose—a half a century old—looking as fresh as when Sylvia Ward had first given it to her lover. It was scarcely in full bloom. Some of its **fragile** red leaves curled around its moist center. Two or three dewdrops sparkled in the middle.

"That is certainly a very pretty **deception**," said the doctor's friends. But they were not too excited. They had seen greater miracles at a magician's show. "Please, tell us how it was done?"

"Have you never heard of the Fountain of Youth?" asked Dr. Heidegger. "The fountain that Ponce de Leon, the Spanish explorer, went in search of two or three centuries ago?"

"But did Ponce de Leon ever find it?" said the Widow Wycherly.

"No," answered Dr. Heidegger. "He never looked for it in the right place. If my information is right, the famous Fountain of Youth is located in the southern part of Florida, not far from Lake Macaco.

"Its source is shaded by several huge magnolias. Those trees are many centuries old. But they have been kept as fresh as violets by the **virtues** of this wonderful water. A friend of mine knows that I am curious about such things. He sent me what you see in the vase."

"Ahem!" said Colonel Killigrew. He did not believe a word of the doctor's story. "And how will this liquid affect the human body?"

"You shall judge for yourself, my dear colonel," replied Dr. Heidegger. "As can all of you, my respected friends. You are welcome to as much of this wonderful liquid as will give you back the bloom of youth.

"As for me, I have had too much trouble in growing old. I am in no hurry to grow young again. So if you will allow me, I will merely watch what happens during the experiment."

While he spoke, Dr. Heidegger had been filling the four champagne glasses with the water of the Fountain of Youth. It seemed to be full of a sparkling gas. Little bubbles were continually rising from the bottoms of the glasses. They burst in silvery spray at the surface.

The liquor gave off a pleasant smell. So the old people did not doubt that it had helpful and comforting qualities. They were complete **skeptics** when it came to believing that it could make them young again. Yet they were ready to swallow it at once. But Dr. Heidegger begged them to wait a moment.

"Before you drink, my respectable old friends, please think," he said. "It would be good if you use your experience of a lifetime to draw up a few general rules. These rules could guide you when you go through the **perils** of youth a second time.

"This would give you a wonderful advantage. Think what a sin and shame it would be if you did not become models of virtue and wisdom for today's young people!"

The only answer from the doctor's four venerable friends was a weak and shaky laugh. The idea that they should ever sin again was ridiculous. They knew how quickly regret follows error.

"Drink, then," said the doctor, bowing. "I rejoice that I have chosen the subjects for my experiment so well."

With shaking hands, they raised the glasses to their lips. If the liquor really had the virtues Dr. Heidegger said it did, it could not have been given to four more needy humans. They looked as if they had never known what youth or pleasure was. They appeared to be the children of Nature's old age.

The gray, worn-out, lifeless, miserable creatures now sat stooping over the doctor's table. They did not have enough life in their souls or bodies to be excited even by the thought of growing young again.

They drank the water and put their glasses down on the table.

Certainly the guests looked better almost immediately. The change was like that made by a large glass of wine along with a sudden glow of cheerful sunshine. At once their faces brightened. There was now a healthy color in their cheeks. The paleness that had made them look so much like **corpses** was gone.

They gazed at one another. They began to think that some magic power had really begun to work. Something seemed to be smoothing away the deep, sad lines which Father Time had been drawing on their foreheads for so long. The Widow Wycherly adjusted her cap. She felt almost like a woman again.

"Give us more of this wonderful water!" they cried eagerly. "We are younger—but we are still too old! Quick—give us more!"

"Patience, patience!" said Dr. Heidegger. He sat watching the experiment with thoughtful coolness. "It has taken you a long time to grow old. Surely you should be happy to grow young in half an hour! But the water is yours to drink whenever you please."

Again he filled their glasses with the liquor of youth.

Enough was still left in the vase to make half the old people in the city as young as their grandchildren.

While the bubbles were still sparkling at the brim, the doctor's guests snatched up their glasses. They all swallowed the contents in a single gulp.

Was it their imagination? Even while they were swallowing the drink, it seemed to change their whole systems. Their eyes grew clear and bright. Their silvery hair grew darker. They sat around the table, three gentlemen of middle age and a woman hardly beyond her blooming **prime**.

"My dear widow, you are charming!" cried Colonel Killigrew. He had been staring at her face. He had seen the shadows of age flit from her like darkness from the red dawn.

From her experience, the lovely widow knew that Colonel Killigrew's compliments were not always truthful. So she jumped up and ran to the mirror. She still feared that the ugly face of an old woman would meet her gaze.

Meanwhile, the three gentlemen acted in a way which proved that the water of the Fountain of Youth had some **intoxicating** qualities. Or perhaps they were just lighthearted and dizzy from suddenly growing young again.

Mr. Gascoigne seemed to be thinking about political topics. But it was not easy to decide if he was thinking about the past, present, or future. After all, the same ideas and phrases had been popular for the past fifty years.

Now he rattled out booming sentences about **patriotism**, national glory, and the people's rights. Now he muttered some perilous stuff in a sly and uncertain whisper. He did this so carefully that even his own conscience could scarcely catch the secret. Now again his voice became poetic and deeply respectful. He spoke as if a king were listening to his well-shaped sentences.

All this time, Colonel Killigrew had been singing a jolly bottle song. He rang his glass in time with the chorus.[4]

---

[4]The chorus is a part of a song that is repeated at the end of each verse.

Meanwhile, he kept glancing at the shapely figure of the Widow Wycherly.

On the other side of the table, Mr. Medbourne was busy adding up dollars and cents. His figuring was strangely linked to a plan to supply the East Indies with ice by hooking a team of whales to the polar icebergs.

As for the Widow Wycherly, she stood before the mirror making a curtsy and smiling at her own image. She greeted it like a friend whom she loved better than all the world.

She pushed her face close to the glass. She wanted to see if some long-remembered wrinkle or crowsfoot[5] was really gone. She checked to see whether the snow had entirely melted from her hair. She wanted to find out if she could safely throw away the venerable cap. At last, turning quickly away, she came to the table with a dancing step.

"My dear old doctor," she cried, "please give me another glass!"

"Certainly, my dear lady, certainly!" replied the willing doctor. "See! I have already filled the glasses."

In fact, there stood the four glasses, brimming with this wonderful water. The airy spray looked like the glitter of diamonds as it bubbled from the surface.

It was now so close to sunset that the room had grown darker than ever. But a mild and moonlike gleam shone from within the vase. It rested on all four guests as well as on the doctor's venerable figure.

He sat in a high-backed armchair with elaborate carvings. The dignity of his gray face might have suited Father Time, whose power had never been **disputed** except by this lucky group. Even as they took their third drink, the guests were almost frightened by the look on his mysterious face.

But the next moment, the exciting gush of young life shot through their veins. They were now in the happy prime of youth. The miserable cares, sorrows, and diseases of age

---

[5]A crowsfoot is a skin wrinkle at the edge of the eye.

were past. These troubles were remembered only as a bad dream from which they had joyfully awakened.

They had lost the fresh glow of youth early in life. Without that glow, their experiences through the years had been just a collection of faded pictures. Now that freshness returned and again threw its magic over all their hopes. They felt like newly created beings in a newly created universe.

"We are young! We are young!" they cried rejoicing.

In their old age, they had all seemed alike. Now youth had erased the individual traits they had in middle age. Once again, they all seemed alike. They were a group of merry youngsters, almost maddened with lively playfulness.

Their most remarkable change was an **impulse** to make fun of how weak and feeble they had been just lately. They laughed loudly at their old-fashioned clothes. The young men's flared coats and flapped vests seemed funny. And the ancient cap and gown of the blooming young girl amused them, too.

One of them limped across the floor like a grandfather with gout. One set a pair of glasses on his nose. He pretended to read the pages of the book of magic. A third sat in an armchair and tried to imitate the venerable dignity of Dr. Heidegger. Then they all shouted merrily and leaped about the room.

The Widow Wycherly—if so fresh a girl could be called a widow—danced up to the doctor's chair. She had a **mischievous**, merry look on her rosy face.

"Doctor, you dear old soul," she cried, "get up and dance with me!"

And then the four young people laughed louder than ever. They thought how strange the poor old doctor would look.

"Please excuse me," answered the doctor quietly. "I am old and stiff. My dancing days were over long ago. But any of these happy, young gentlemen will be glad to have so pretty a partner."

"Dance with me, Clara!" cried Colonel Killigrew.

"No, no, I will be her partner!" shouted Mr. Gascoigne.

"She promised to marry me fifty years ago!" exclaimed Mr. Medbourne.

They all gathered round her. One grabbed both her hands with passion. Another threw his arm around her waist. The third buried his hand among the shining curls **clustered** beneath her cap.

The widow blushed, panted, struggled, scolded, and laughed. Her warm breath fanned each of their faces as she tried to free herself. Yet she still remained in their triple embrace. Never was there a livelier picture of youthful competition. And charming beauty was the prize.

Yet a strange deception occurred. Perhaps it was due to the darkness of the room and the old clothes which they still wore. At any rate, the tall mirror is said to have reflected the figures of three old, gray, withered grandfathers. They were seen to be in a ridiculous fight for a skinny, ugly, withered grandmother.

But they were young. Their burning passions proved that was true. The girl-widow flirted, which drove the three rivals mad. She would not give them her affection or withhold it. They began to exchange **threatening** glances. Still keeping hold of the fair prize, they grabbed fiercely at one another's throats.

As they struggled back and forth, the table was tipped over. The vase smashed into a thousand pieces. The valuable Water of Youth flowed in a bright stream across the floor.

This water splashed the wings of a butterfly. It had grown old, now that it was the end of summer, and had landed there to die. The insect fluttered lightly through the room and settled on the snowy head of Dr. Heidegger.

"Come, come, gentlemen! Come, Mrs. Wycherly," exclaimed the doctor, "I really must protest against this riot."

They stood still and shivered. It seemed as if gray Time

were calling them back from their sunny youth. They were being summoned far down into the cold, dark world of old age.

They looked at old Dr. Heidegger, who sat in his carved armchair. He held the rose that was a half a century old. He had rescued it from the pieces of the broken vase.

At the motion of his hand, the four rioters sat down again. They did so willingly. Their wild efforts had tired them, though they were young.

"My poor Sylvia's rose!" exclaimed Dr. Heidegger. He held it up in the light of the sunset clouds. "It appears to be fading again."

And so it was. Even while the group looked at it, the flower continued to wither. Finally it became as dry and fragile as when the doctor had first thrown it into the vase. He shook off the few drops of water which clung to its petals.

"I love it as well like this as when it was fresh," he noted. He pressed the withered rose to his withered lips. While he spoke, the butterfly fluttered down from the doctor's snowy head. It fell upon the floor.

His guests shivered again. They all felt that a strange chill was slowly creeping over them. But whether the chill was in their bodies or spirits, they could not tell.

They gazed at one another. And they imagined that each moment that sped past snatched away some of the magic. In its place, a deepening wrinkle appeared where none had been before.

Was it a dream? Had the changes of a lifetime been crowded into such a brief time? Were they now four old people, sitting with their old friend, Dr. Heidegger?

"Have we grown old again, so soon?" they cried sadly.

Indeed, they had. The virtues of the Water of Youth passed away even faster than those of wine. The **delirium** which it created had bubbled away.

Yes! they were old again. The widow shuddered with an impulse that showed she still was a woman. She put her skinny hands over her face. She wished that the coffin lid were over it, since it could not be beautiful any longer.

"Yes, friends, you are old again," said Dr. Heidegger. "And see—the Water of Youth is all wasted on the ground!

"Well, I am not sorry. If the fountain gushed at my doorstep, I would not bend down to wash my lips in it. No, not even if the delirium lasted for years instead of moments. That is the lesson you have taught me!"

But the doctor's four friends had not learned that lesson. They decided at once to make a trip to Florida. There they would drink from the Fountain of Youth at morning, noon, and night.

"Dr. Heidegger's Experiment" was first published in 1837.

INSIGHTS INTO
NATHANIEL HAWTHORNE

(1804-1864)

Among Hawthorne's ancestors were William Hathorne and John Hathorne. (Nathaniel added a "w" to the family name.) William Hathorne was a colonist who persecuted Quakers. John Hathorne was a judge at the Salem witch trials. These hard-hearted Puritans helped spark Hawthorne's interest in sin, evil, and guilt.

After college, Hawthorne went to Salem to live with his mother and sisters. There he remained shut up for twelve lonely years, writing. Finally his book *Twice-Told Tales* was published in 1837. Hawthorne said that at last, "FAME was won." Actually, fame was still to come. But Hawthorne's career as a writer had begun.

Hawthorne tried for years to become a well-known writer. At times he felt gloomy about his chance for success. So when James Fields offered to publish a book of Hawthorne's, the author was amazed. He asked, "Who would risk publishing a book for *me,* the most unimportant writer in America?" Fields said he would. As a result, *The Scarlet Letter* was printed. Fields' confidence was repaid. The book sold 5,000 copies within ten days.

Hawthorne counted many famous people among his friends. Herman Melville, who wrote *Moby Dick,* was Hawthorne's neighbor. Franklin Pierce, fourteenth president of the United States, was Hawthorne's lifelong friend. In fact, Pierce was on vacation with Hawthorne when the author died. Writers

continued

Longfellow, Holmes, Whittier, Lowell, and Emerson went to Hawthorne's funeral. Yet Hawthorne thought of himself as "the obscurest man of letters in America."

Other works by Hawthorne:
"The Ambitious Guest," short story
"The Birthmark," short story
"The Minister's Black Veil," short story
"My Kinsman, Major Molineux," short story
"Rappaccini's Daughter," short story
"Young Goodman Brown," short story
The House of the Seven Gables, novel
The Scarlet Letter, novel